学术顾问
（以姓氏笔画为序）

王　宏　　冯智文　　李正栓　　李丽生　　原一川

Academic Advisors
Wang Hong　　Feng Zhiwen　　Li Zhengshuan

Li Lisheng　　Yuan Yichuan

主　编
李昌银

副主编
黄　瑛　　彭庆华

General Editor
Li Changyin

Professor of English Yunnan Normal University

Associate General Editors
Huang Ying

Professor of English Yunnan Normal University

Peng Qinghua

Professor of English Yunnan Normal University

云南少数民族经典作品英译文库
Classics of Yunnan Ethnic Groups in English Translation

主编 李昌银　General Editor　Li Changyin
副主编 黄瑛 彭庆华　Associate General Editors　Huang Ying & Peng Qinghua

Twelve Nujus
十二奴局

搜集整理◎赵官禄　郭纯礼
　　　　　黄世荣　梁福生
英译◎王蕾
译校◎[美]包琼

Collected & Edited by Zhao Guanlu, Guo Chunli,
Huang Shirong & Liang Fusheng
Translated by Wang Lei
Revised by Joan Cecile Bouleric

云南出版集团
云南人民出版社

图书在版编目（CIP）数据

十二奴局：汉、英 / 赵官禄等搜集整理；王蕾英译.——昆明：云南人民出版社，2018.12
（云南少数民族经典作品英译文库 / 李昌银主编）
ISBN 978-7-222-17504-4

Ⅰ.①十… Ⅱ.①赵…②王… Ⅲ.①哈尼族—史诗—中国—汉、英 Ⅳ.①I222.7

中国版本图书馆CIP数据核字(2018)第277428号

出 品 人	李 维	赵石定	
项目统筹	周 祥	殷筱钊	
项目组稿	郭木玉		
责任编辑	郭木玉	任建红	李东华
设计制作	马 滨	三人禾	
责任校对	卫佳睿	崔苡菡	付芳侠 周桉吉
责任印制	陆卫华	代隆参	

云南少数民族经典作品英译文库
Classics of Yunnan Ethnic Groups in English Translation

十二奴局
Twelve Nujus

搜集整理◎赵官禄 郭纯礼 黄世荣 梁福生
英译◎王蕾
译校◎[美]包琼

Collected & Edited by Zhao Guanlu, Guo Chunli,
Huang Shirong & Liang Fusheng
Translated by Wang Lei
Revised by Joan Cecile Bouleric

出 版	云南出版集团 云南人民出版社
发 行	云南人民出版社
社 址	昆明市环城西路609号
邮 编	650034
网 址	www.ynpph.com.cn
E-mail	ynrms@sina.com
开 本	787mm×1092mm 1/16
印 张	15.25
字 数	250千
版 次	2018年12月第1版第1次印刷
印 刷	云南出版印刷（集团）有限责任公司 云南新华印刷一厂
书 号	ISBN 978-7-222-17504-4
定 价	85.00元

云南人民出版社
公众微信号

序 一

◎李正栓

民族典籍英译是传播中国文化、文学和文明的重要途径，是中华文化走出去的重要组成部分。文化与文学的传播，是一个国家提高文化软实力的重要方式，在文化交流和文明建设中起着不可或缺的作用，对提高国家对外话语权、构建国家对外话语体系以及对建设世界文学都有积极意义。

中国各少数民族拥有许多优秀的典籍，具有很高的文物价值、文学价值和文化价值。各民族的先人们通过口头流传或用文字记述了他们各具特色的文化。各少数民族几乎都有自己民族的创世史、史诗和神话传说。

中国民族典籍独具特色，不可替代。重视民族典籍的翻译和研究工作，对于挖掘各民族优秀文化，保护各民族文明，增强各民族之间的沟通和了解，进一步向世界其他地区传播各少数民族优秀文化，乃至提高我国文化软实力都有着重要意义。不少少数民族聚居地处于祖国边疆，有的处在"一带一路"建设关键部位，有的处在与周边国家进行各种交流的重要位置。

中国民族典籍是世界多元文化的有机组成部分，与其他文化共同造就了世界文化的绚丽多姿。世界正因为其文化多样性才变得缤纷多彩。我国各民族典籍中包含的文化多样性极大地丰富了世界多元、特色鲜明的文化。人们对多样性形成全新的认识角度和思维方式。多样性开阔了人们的视野，丰富了人们思考问题的角度。挖掘这些典籍中所蕴含的教育价值和文化价值，对世界其他民族都有指导和借鉴意义，并且有助于建设我国的文化自信。

民族典籍本身蕴含的特殊价值对加强民族文化了解、促进中外文化交流具有重大意义。民族典籍英译具有文学翻译和文化传递之功能，有对外宣传作用，还是一种文学外交。因此，民族典籍翻译和研究对于维护祖国统一、促进民族团结、稳定边疆以及增强国内各民族和中外文化之间的交流都起着极为重要的作用。

中华人民共和国成立以后，中央政府一直十分重视民族典籍翻译和研究工作，提供了强有力的政策支持，并采取了一系列有效措施，加快了各少数民族典籍的抢救、整理、翻译和研究的进程。中央政府多次召开西藏工作会议和新疆工作会议。近年来，国际和国内对于多元文化高度关注，少数民族文学典籍的翻译已然成为业内研究的热点。

近年来，民族典籍翻译和研究迅猛发展，势头良好。国家大力支持，发放国家社科基金课题，教育部和国家民委也发放课题，扶持了一大批研究者。很多民族典籍翻译课题得以立项并顺利开展；为数不少的民族典籍被翻译成汉语、英语和其他语言并出版发行；越来越多的业界人士致力于这个满富生机的学术领域。

在中国文化走出去的国家战略下，全国少数民族典籍英译学术研讨会陆续召开，已经召开三次。

云南是中国民族最多的省份。人口在 5000 人以上的少数民族有 25 个，其中有 15 个民族为云南所特有，分别是：白族、哈尼族、傣族、傈僳族、佤族、拉祜族、纳西族、景颇族、布朗族、普米族、阿昌族、基诺族、怒族、德昂族、独龙族。其中除白族人口占全国白族人口总数的 84% 以上外，其他 14 个民族 95% 居住在云南。

云南还是我国跨境民族最多的省份。在云南的 25 个少数民族中，有 16 个民族跨境而居，分别是：傣族、壮族、苗族、景颇族、瑶族、哈尼族、德昂族、佤族、拉祜族、彝族、阿昌族、傈僳族、布依族、怒族、布朗族、独龙族。

云南少数民族创造了辉煌的文化。据不完全统计，云南少数民族文字文献古籍蕴藏量达 10 万余册（卷），口传古籍 4 万余种。云南省民委少数民族古籍整理出版规划办公室为了挽救和保护这些古籍，计划在 5 年内编纂出版 100 卷《云南少数民族古籍珍本集成》。这是一个令人瞩目的庞大计划。将这些古籍中的珍品翻译介绍给世界，不仅能够弘扬云南省丰富多彩的民族文化，而且有助于增进与南亚东南亚国家的理解与交流，为"一带一路"倡议的实施做出贡献。

云南师范大学外国语学院很重视这一领域的工作。在外国语学院领导支持下，李昌银教授带领一个由教授和中青年学者组成的团队对精选出来的 17 部云南少数民族经典作品进行英译，计划在 5 年内（"十三五"期间）翻译出版。这是一项十分有意义的宏大工程。

这 17 部民族典籍，内容全部为各民族的英雄史诗或神话传说，具有很高的历史意义和文学价值。这些作品涉及阿昌族、白族、傣族、德昂族、哈尼族、景颇族、拉祜族、苗族、纳西族、普米族、彝族等 11 个少数民族。

云南师范大学这支翻译队伍实力强大，主要由一些多年从事翻译教学、研究和实践的教授和副教授组成，他们是李昌银、黄瑛、彭庆华、孙兴文、吴相如、刘德周、杨慧芳、郜菊、陈萍、包琼（Joan Boulerice）等国内外专家学者。他们在云南翻译界都是风云人物。

在民族典籍英译中，这支队伍异军突起，为我国民族典籍英译壮大了声势，必将为中国民族典籍走向世界而成为世界文学的一部分做出新贡献。

民族典籍翻译与研究事业关乎国家的稳定统一，关乎民族关系的和谐发展，关乎世界多元文化的实现。在中国，民族典籍资源极为丰富，有待进一步挖掘、翻译。因此，民族典籍英译前景光明。同时，我们也应意识到，仍有许多濒临消失的少数民族典籍亟待拯救，民族典籍翻译与研究工作任重而道远。

（李正栓，中国英汉语比较研究会典籍英译专业委员会常务副会长兼秘书长）

Foreword by Li Zhengshuan

The translation of Chinese ethnic classics is an important approach in spreading Chinese culture, literature and civilization. It is a crucial component of Chinese culture going global. The spreading of Chinese culture and literature is a national policy and an important way to improve the cultural soft power of China. It plays an indispensable role in the cultural exchange between China and other countries and the development of world literature.

The ethnic groups in China have countless excellent classics with high anthropological, literary and cultural value. The ancestors of each ethnic group have passed down their distinctive culture orally or in writing. Almost all the ethnic groups have their own story of creation, epics, myths and legends.

Chinese ethnic classics are unique and irreplaceable. It is imperative to attach importance to the translation and research of ethnic classics; to explore the excellent ethnic cultures; to protect the civilization of ethnic groups; to enhance the communication and understanding among ethnic groups; to further spread the outstanding culture of ethnic groups to other parts of the world; and to build the cultural strength of China. Many ethnic groups live in the border areas and thus play an important role in the cultural and economic cooperation between China and its neighbors in the context of the Belt and Road Initiative.

Chinese ethnic classics are an important component of the magnificence and diversity of world culture. It is diversity that makes the world so colorful. The cultural diversity of Chinese ethnic classics has greatly enriched the world's pluralism and its distinctive features. People around the world have formed a new understanding of diversity. This diversity has expanded people's horizon and enriched their way of thinking. Digging out the educational and cultural value in these classics can contribute to the construction of China's self-confidence in culture.

The special value of the ethnic classics itself is of great significance to the strengthening of national culture and intercultural communication between China and foreign countries. The translation of ethnic classics is not just a literary exchange, but also a form of cultural communication. It is diplomacy through literature in that it consolidates the cultural ties between China and other countries.

After the founding of the People's Republic of China, the central government attached great importance to the translation and research of ethnic classics, provided the a great deal of policy support, and adopted a series of effective measures to speed up the process of rescuing, collating, translating and studying ethnic classics. The central government has convened several working conferences on Tibet and Xinjiang. In recent years, both China and other countries have paid close attention to multiculture. The translation of ethnic classics has become a hot topic.

In recent years, the translation and research of ethnic classics have progressed rapidly and have shown good prospects. The government strongly supports and grants the research projects of the national social science fund. The Ministry of Education and the State Ethnic Affairs Commission are also issuing research projects and giving funding to a large number of researchers. Many research projects on ethnic classics have been approved and carried out. Many ethnic classics have been translated into Chinese, English and other languages and published. More and more professionals have dedicated themselves to this new sphere of learning.

In this context, the academic conferences on translation of ethnic classics are held one after another all around the country. And up to now three have been held.

Yunnan is the province which has the most ethnic groups in China. Besides Han people, there are 25 ethnic groups, each with a population of more than 5,000. Among them, 15 ethnic groups are unique to Yunnan, which are the Bai, the Hani, the Dai, the Lisu, the Wa, the Lahu, the Naxi, the Jingpo, the Bulang, the Pumi, the Achang, the Jinuo, the Nu, the De'ang and the Dulong. Among these, 84% of the total number of the Bai people in China and 95% of the other 14 ethnic groups are living in Yunnan.

Yunnan is also the province which has the most cross-border ethnic groups. Of the 25 ethnic groups, 16 live across the border, namely: the Dai, the Zhuang, the Miao, the Jingpo, the Yao, the Hani, the De'ang, the Wa, the Lahu, the Yi, the Achang, the Lisu, the Buyi, the Nu, the Bulang and the Dulong.

The ethnic groups in Yunnan have created splendid cultures. According to statistics, the number of classics of Yunnan ethnic groups is more than 100 thousand volumes and classics in oral tradition are more than 40 thousand. In order to save and protect these ancient books, the Office of Classics Collation and Publishing of Yunnan Ethnic Groups Affairs Commission planned to compile and publish 100 volumes of *A Collection of Yunnan Ethnic Group Rare Books* in five years, which is an ambitious plan. The introduction of the ancient classics via translation can not only promote and develop the colorful ethnic cultures of Yunnan, but also contribute to the understanding and exchange between China and countries in South Asia and Southeast Asia and to the implementation of the Belt and Road Initiative as well.

The School of Foreign Languages and Literature of Yunnan Normal University is paying close attention to this field. With the support of the School and the University, Professor Li Changyin is leading a group of professors and young scholars to do the project of *"Classics of Yunnan Ethnic Groups in English Translation"*, which includes 17 ethnic classics selected carefully from Yunnan's bountiful ethnic classics. These books are the heroic epics or myths and legends of each ethnic groups with great historical significance and literary value. They will finish the translation in five years (during "the thirteenth five-year plan"). After that, all the works will be published by Yunnan People's Publishing House.

The 17 works cover 11 ethnic groups: the Achang, the Bai, the Dai, the De'ang, the Hani, the Jingpo, the Lahu, the Miao, the Naxi, the Pumi and the Yi. All of these groups except the Miao and the Yi are unique to Yunnan.

The translation team of Yunnan Normal University is full of strength and vitality, composed of professors and associate professors who have been occupied in translation teaching, research, and practice for a long time. They are Li Changyin, Huang Ying, Peng Qinghua, Sun Xingwen, Wu Xiangru, Liu Dezhou, Yang Huifang, Gao Ju, Chen Ping, Joan Boulerice and other experts and scholars who are representative figures in the translation field in Yunnan province.

This team is a new force that has suddenly arisen in terms of translating ethnic classics. It is expanding the momentum of ethnic classics translation in China and has made a new contribution for China's ethnic classics to go global and become a part of world literature.

The translation and research of ethnic classics are related to the development of Chinese culture and the realization of multiculturalism in the world. In China, ethnic classics are extremely rich in resources, which require us to make further exploration and research and translate them into other languages. Therefore, the future of translating ethnic classics is bright. At the same time, we should also realize that there are still many ethnic works which are close to extinction and urgently need to be rescued. We still have a long way to go in the fields of translation and research in ethnic classics.

(Li Zhengshuan, Standing Vice Chairman and Secretary General, Classics Translation Committee of CACSEC)

序 二

◎王 宏

  好友云南师范大学外国语学院李昌银教授来电嘱托我为"云南少数民族经典作品英译文库"的出版写一序言，并随即发来该文库的背景资料，让我"不着急，慢慢写"。我本人从事中国典籍英译及研究，深知少数民族典籍对外传译的重要性，但又是少数民族典籍翻译的门外汉。因此，我是怀着虚心学习的态度来写此序言的。近年来，在中国文化"走出去"战略工程大背景下，在中央和地方各级政府的大力支持下，我国少数民族典籍的对外传译及研究工作顺利开展，取得了很大的进步。请看以下数据：

  2008年，广西百色学院韩家权教授获批国家社科基金项目《布洛陀史诗》（壮汉英对照）。该项目已顺利结项，并于2013年12月获得中国民间文艺最高奖"山花奖"。

  2012年，广西百色学院外语系翻译团队翻译的国家级非物质文化遗产《壮族嘹歌》（英文版）由广西师范大学出版社正式出版。

  2012年，东北大学秦皇岛分校吴松林教授主编的《蒙古族系列：江格尔（汉英对照）》（上下册）由吉林大学出版社出版。

  2013年，河北师范大学李正栓教授英译《藏族格言诗》

由长春出版社出版发行。

2013年，云南财经大学崔晓霞教授撰写的《〈阿诗玛〉英译研究》收入由王宏印教授主编、民族出版社出版的"民族典籍翻译研究丛书"。

2014年，东北大学秦皇岛分校吴松林教授撰写的《满族档案文献研究》申请到国家社科后期资助，他英译的《英雄格斯尔可汗》由吉林大学出版社出版。

2014年，中南民族大学张立玉教授主持的"土家族主要典籍英译及研究"获批国家社科基金项目。

2015年，西安外国语大学梁真惠副教授撰写的《〈玛纳斯〉翻译传播研究》收入由王宏印教授主编、民族出版社出版的"民族典籍翻译研究丛书"。

与此同时，第一届和第二届全国少数民族典籍英译学术研讨会分别于2012年和2014年在广西民族大学和大连民族学院举行，参加会议的院校分布之广、与会代表数量之众、提交论文数量之多和涉及研究话题之细，十分可喜。2016年还将在中南民族大学举行第三届全国少数民族典籍英译学术研讨会。

为什么少数民族典籍的对外传译及研究工作在短短几年就受到译界的青睐，取得众多成果？我认为，这在很大程度上归于典籍翻译界乃至翻译界同仁对"中国典籍"的重新思考和认识。中国典籍浩如烟海，卷帙浩繁，举世瞩目，是全人类共同的精神财富。但对于中国典籍的理解，我们以前较多限于汉民族的重要文献和书籍，而对少数民族多有忽略。在讨论中国典籍时，也较多关注古代文学作品。其实，中国典籍指"中国清代末年1911年以前的重要文献和书籍",这就要求我们从事典籍翻译时,不但要翻译古代文学典籍作品,还要翻译古代哲学、科技、法律、医学、经济、军事、天文、地理等诸多方面的典籍作品,不但要翻译汉民族的典籍作品,也要翻译各少数民族的典籍作品。

民族典籍具有该民族的原型符号的特质,蕴藏着能够"遗传"并不断"再生"的文化基因。民族典籍是中华传统文化的内核,同时还是中华传统文化的符号构成规则。中国是具有56个民族的多民族国家,少数民族典籍是我国少数民族勤劳与智慧的结晶,是中华文明、也是世界文明不可或缺的一部分。少数民族典籍对外传译具有跨文化交流的作用,它不但有助于更多的人了解少数民族的独特文化,而且还有助于保护少数民族文化的独特性、维持少数民族文化多样性、促进各民族团结、提升中华文化软实力等。

中国少数民族典籍涉及宗教、文学、历史、语言、医学、天文历算等领域,内容丰富,版本多样,载体特殊,传承奇特。仅以《中国少数民族古籍总目提要》为例,该书于1997年正式立项,全书总体设计约60卷、110册,目前已出版23个民族卷共20册:纳西族卷、白族卷、东乡族卷·裕固族卷·保安族卷、土族卷·撒拉族卷、锡伯族卷、哈尼族卷、回族卷·铭刻、柯尔克孜族卷、羌族卷、毛南族卷·京族卷、仫佬族卷、达斡尔族卷、土家族卷、鄂温克族卷、鄂伦春族卷、赫哲族卷、苗族卷、侗族卷、黎族卷、朝鲜族卷。该书真实地反映了我国各少数民族古籍赋存的全面情况,充实了中国的历史和文化内容,为后人探索各种文化形式的源流、揭示中国社会文化发展的轨迹提供了极为珍贵的资料,为我国乃至世界各国人文科学研究提供了一套新颖而全面的资料,对于弘扬中华民族传统文化具有深远的历史意义和现实意义。

少数民族典籍的对外传译是一项艰巨的工作，涉及将少数民族语言译成汉语、少数民族语言之间的互译和少数民族语言译成外语（主要是英语）。前两类翻译历史源远流长，最早可追溯到春秋战国时代《越人歌》的翻译，即汉、壮语之间的翻译。少数民族典籍译成外语的时间则要晚一些。据考证，维吾尔族古典长诗《福乐智慧》成书于1069年或1070年，目前尚未发现完整的原稿，只存留下来三个抄本，分别为赫拉特抄本、费尔干纳抄本与埃及抄本，其中费尔干纳抄本于12~13世纪用阿拉伯文纳斯赫体抄写，1914年发现于今中亚乌孜别克斯坦纳曼干城，现存于该共和国科学院东方研究所。这是少数民族典籍译介到国外的最早纪录。少数民族典籍外译在现代有了较快发展。一些少数民族典籍，如藏族的《格萨尔王传》、蒙古族的《江格尔》和柯尔克孜族的《玛纳斯》等英雄史诗，云南彝族的《阿诗玛》、维吾尔族的《艾里甫和赛乃姆》等民间叙事长诗已先后被翻译成英语及其他外国文字，为世人所知。这对传承少数民族经典，推动中外文化交流起到了不可替代的作用。然而，还有大量的中国少数民族典籍等待我们去翻译和研究。

云南省少数民族典籍资源十分丰富。据不完全统计，云南少数民族文字文献古籍蕴藏量达10万余册（卷），口传古籍4万余种。"云南少数民族经典作品英译文库"正是依托云南省丰富的少数民族典籍资源，借助云南师范大学外国语学院强大的翻译师资队伍，在云南人民出版社的有力支持下，首次将云南少数民族经典作品成系列对外译介的大力举措。云南师范大学外国语学院对"云南少数民族经典作品英译文库"十分重视，他们首先邀请省内外少数民族语言文化研究专家对云南民族典籍和民族文化经典作品进行筛选，做到"好中选好，优中选优"，同时调配最强的翻译力量承担文库的翻译任务。我粗略看了该文库的选题，发现选题面广，覆盖范围宽，收入了云南省阿昌族、白族、傣族、纳西族、德昂族、哈尼族、景颇族、拉祜族、苗族、普米族和彝族等民族的典籍作品。云南共有25个少数民族，其中11个少数民族的典籍作品都覆盖到了，不少作品还是首次译成英文。这将彻底改变云南少数民族典籍由于对外译介数量较少，不为世界了解的尴尬局面。

对于云南师范大学外国语学院而言，把少数民族典籍英译作为翻译专业的优势特色进行建设，这将对该院的学科建设起到助推作用。"云南少数民族经典作品英译文库"所产生的翻译成果和研究成果将培养出一批优秀的典籍翻译和研究团队，凸显该院在全国的学术特色和学术影响，同时还能将翻译能力和研究能力转化为教学能力，提高云南师范大学外国语学院翻译专业研究生的培养质量，为社会输送高水平的翻译人才，有力地支撑学院翻译专业学科的建设和发展。我对云南师范大学外国语学院的翻译师资队伍较为熟悉。作为云南省唯一获得省级高校优势特色学科建设项目的外国语学院，该院具有雄厚的翻译师资力量，在云南省各高校中当属第一。多年来，该院翻译与跨文化研究团队一直承担着对外交流与合作的各种口笔译项目及任务。由外国语学院精心挑选和确定的"云南少数民族经典作品英译文库"翻译人员绝大多数都是云南省翻译领域里的知名教授或专家，有国外留学经历，且具有扎实的英汉双语语言功底，曾翻译出版多部译著和翻译作品，并且主持和参与过多项翻译项目的研究。我阅读李昌银教授发来的文库翻译人员名单，发现多名我所熟悉的知名教授、博士也在其中，感到格外放心。

"云南少数民族经典作品英译文库"的出版发行是云南省翻译界的一件大事，也是我国少数民族典籍翻译传来的又一佳音。想当年，我和《大中华文库》总协调人李林老师曾在参加全国典籍英译学术研讨会之余一起找到李昌银教授，敦促李教授向学校和同事呼吁，少数民族典籍翻译及研究是富矿，值得快挖、深挖，能早出成果，出大成果。今天，我们当年的心愿变成了美好的现实，心里感到特别高兴。再次热烈祝贺"云南少数民族经典作品英译文库"的顺利出版！

（王宏，中国典籍翻译研究会副会长、苏州大学博士生导师）

Foreword by Wang Hong

My friend Professor Li Changyin of Yunnan Normal University asked me to write a few words for the publication of *Classics of Yunnan Ethnic Groups in English Translation*. I am more than delighted to do it. As I have been doing research in the English translation of Chinese classics, I know how important his work is. In recent years, substantial progress has been made in translating Chinese ethnic classics into English and other foreign languages. Books published in this respect include *The Liao Songs of the Zhuang Nationality* (Nanning: Guangxi Normal University Press, 2008, English Edition), *Mongolian Series: Jianggeer* (Changchun: Jilin University Press, 2012, Bilingual Edition), *Tibetan Gnomic Verses Translated into English* (Changchun: Changchun Press, 2013), and *Geser Khan: a Hero* (Changchun: Jilin University Press, 2014). Several projects in the English translation of ethnic classics have received funding from the National Planning Office of Philosophy and Social Science and, as a result, a number of monographs and PhD dissertations have been published.

Meanwhile, it is encouraging to see that the first conferences on English translation of ethnic classics in China have been held in Guangxi Nationalities University and

Dalian Nationalities Institute respectively. Participants were both many and enthusiastic. Many papers were presented and a lot of topics discussed. The third conference will be hosted by South Central Nationalities University in 2016.

Why, then, has this field attracted so much attention from translators and scholars alike and accomplished so much in just a few years? The answer, I believe, lies in a rethinking of what constitutes Chinese classics as an indispensable part of human heritage. We used to see Chinese classics as more or less equal to the classics of the Han people, excluding works by other ethnic groups. Moreover, when we talk about Chinese classics, we focus too much on the literary works of ancient times. Yet Chinese classics actually refer to "important works and books before 1911, the year when the Qing dynasty fell, bringing an end to imperial rule." This definition requires us to pay attention not just to literary works, but also writings in other subjects, such as philosophy, science, law, medicine, economics, military affairs, astronomy, and geography, not only Han works, but writings by other ethnic groups as well.

The classical works of a nation are its archetypal symbols, the major carriers of its cultural genes. Chinese classics make up the core of Chinese tradition. The Chinese nation consists of 56 ethnic groups. Ethnic classics are an important part of not only Chinese traditional culture, but also of world civilization. The translation of these works into other languages is important in that it helps to promote cross-cultural communications between China and other countries and to protect and preserve the uniqueness and diversity of ethnic cultures by making them accessible to foreign readers.

Chinese ethnic classics cover a variety of areas, such as religion, literature, history, language, medicine, astrology, and calendar, with numerous editions, special media and unique ways of transmission from generation to generation. Take, for example, *An Anthology of Chinese Ethnic Classics*, a colossal project that includes 110 volumes, 20 of which, from 23 ethnic groups, have been published. The anthology reflects the variety and quantity of China's ethnic classics and provides valuable material and resources for studying, understanding and developing Chinese culture and history in a more comprehensive and sustainable way.

The translation of Chinese ethnic classics into foreign languages is a very demanding job, involving rendering from ethnic languages to Chinese, between ethnic languages, and from ethnic languages (often via Chinese) to foreign languages. The first two types of translation can be traced back to the Spring and Autumn Period, when *The Song of the Yue People* was translated from their mother tongue into Chinese. The earliest translation of ethnic classics into a foreign language is *Wisdom of Royal Glory*, a long poem of the Uygurs, which was rendered from the source language into Arabic and is now in the Oriental Institute of Uzbekistan at Namangan. But it was not until modern times that the translation of ethnic classics into foreign languages accelerated. Noticeably, ethnic epics, such as *The Story of Prince Geser* of the Tibetans, *The Story of Jianggeer* of the Mongolians, *Manas* of the Kyrgyz, and narrative poems such as *Ashima* of the Yi people, *Alip and Salam* of the Uygurs, etc., have been published. These translations have contributed to acquainting the world with Chinese ethnic classics, but many remain to be translated.

Yunnan is rich in ethnic classics, boasting more than 100 thousand volumes of written classics and over 40 thousand pieces of oral literature. Relying on such bountiful resources, as a collective endeavor of the translation team of the School of Foreign Languages and Literature, Yunnan Normal University and with the help of Yunnan People's Publishing House, *Classics of Yunnan Ethnic Groups in English Translation* is the first project to translate Yunnan ethnic classics into English on a large scale. The School adheres to a professional spirit and academic standard in carrying out the project by selecting the most authoritative texts in the source language (Chinese) and recruiting the best translators from its huge faculty. The selection of the works, covering eleven of the twenty-five ethnic groups of the province, indicates expertise and insight. The implementation of the project will change the embarrassing obscurity of Yunnan ethnic classics by making them known to the world, many of them for the first time.

In light of disciplinary development, the project is of

great importance, too. Participating in the translation will strengthen the academic foundation of the teachers, enrich their experience and enhance their translation skills and research ability. This in turn will help them become better teachers and thus able to educate students with higher quality. The publication of the books will add greatly to the faculty accomplishments of the School and raise the academic standing of Yunnan Normal University by taking the first step in this direction among the universities of Yunnan province.

This publication project is a great event not only for Yunnan itself, but also for China. Looking back, I remember that Professor Li Changyin, our friend Li Lin, editor of the *Library of Chinese Classics*, and I talked enthusiastically about initiating something like this in Yunnan when we attended a conference on the translation of ethnic classics in Soochow. Lin and I strongly suggested that Professor Li do it as soon as possible. Now I am very pleased to see our talk becoming reality. Again, my congratulations on the publication of *Classics of Yunnan Ethnic Groups in English Translation*!

(Wang Hong, PhD supervisor at Soochow University, Vice Chairman of Classics Translation Committee of CACSEC)

General Introduction

This publication project, Classics of *Yunnan Ethnic Groups in English Translation*, aims at introducing Yunnan ethnic classical works to the world by making them available to native speakers of English who might be interested in them. With the publication of the *Library of Chinese Classics*, which consists only of books written by Han authors in classical Chinese, attention now is being turned to the English translation and publication of ethnic classics, books produced by ethnic writers about their history and culture. Universities in provinces such as Guangxi, Guizhou, Liaoning, Xinjiang, and Xizang, have taken the initiative. We in Yunnan must do something, because Yunnan has the largest number of ethnic groups in China. 15 of the 25 ethnic groups in the province, the Bai, the Dai, the Hani, the Lisu, the Wa, the Lahu, the Naxi, the Jingpo, the Bulang, the Pumi, the Achang, the Jinuo, the Nu, the De'ang, and the Dulong, live in no other place but Yunnan. The classics of these people, either in their own languages or in Chinese translations, are a great treasure house, which should be accessible to English readers and scholars. But what works should be translated first?

All the 25 ethnic groups in Yunnan have their classics, epics, mythology, creation stories, folksongs, folk drama, mountain songs, and funeral lament lyrics, most of which exist in different versions in different places. According to one estimation, there are more than 100 thousand volumes of them, excluding those in oral form. After a thorough survey and extensive consultations with experts of ethnic studies, we concluded that priority must be given to epics and mythologies, as they reflect an ethnic people's philosophy, history and culture more than anything else by narrating the stories of where and how they think they came from. From many epics and mythologies, we selected 17 of the most authoritative and popular classics representing 11 Yunnan ethnic groups, the Yi, the Bai, the Miao, the Hani, the Lahu, the Naxi, the Jingpo, the Pumi, the Achang, the Dai, and the De'ang. These works are all in Chinese, translated from the original by bilingual scholars whose mother tongue is their own ethnic language and who are fluent and proficient in Chinese. Some were recorded from their oral form at rituals and performances. We did not choose texts written in the ethnic language, not least because it is very hard to find a translator who is skilled in both the ethnic language and English. Moreover, some of the classics in the ethnic language were circulated in various oral forms and fragments. The published Chinese versions have been carefully edited and translated, hence they are more reliable. The next question is: how to translate them?

It happens that all of the 17 works except one are in

verse form, with lines more or less the same length and loose rhymes, but no regular meter. A poem must be rendered into a poem; anything less is unacceptable. So here are the general rules we follow when doing the translation.

One. If the original is verse, the translated text must be verse, too.

Two. Reproduce the ideas and the images of the original as completely as possible.

Three. Reproduce the figures of speech of the original as much as possible.

Four. Do not change the number of lines in a stanza unless absolutely necessary.

Five. Do not use standard meters in English, because the Chinese original does not follow any regular meter. Use the natural rhythm of English instead, but most of the lines should look more or less the same length.

Six. Do not use rhyme unless it comes naturally and is faithful to the content of the original.

What we try to do is, to use Susan Bassnett's words, "transplant the seed", not the tree itself. As for the various aspects of form, particularly meter and end rhyme, we reproduce them when it is possible and abandon them when it is necessary.

Who will do the translations? As this is a collective project of the School of Foreign Languages and Literature of Yunnan Normal University, our team consists of a dozen faculty members and two students from our MA translation program who are already teachers in other universities. All the translators have been teaching translation and doing translation research for a long time. They have published not just academic articles on translation, but also translated books from English to Chinese or vice versa.

Traditionally, people translate into their mother tongue, not into a foreign language. But the situation is changing. Many translators today are translating from their mother tongue into a foreign language. The quality can be good, as Nike K. Pokorn and Stuart Campbell prove in *Challenging the Traditional Axioms: Translation into a non-mother tongue* (Amsterdam: John Benjamins Publishing Company, 2005) and *Translation into the Second Language* (New York: Routledge, 2013) respectively. The case of China provides further evidence for their argument. The translation of Chinese classics into English was initiated by James Legge and Herbert Allen Giles in the 19th century and carried on in the 20th century by Arthur Waley, David Hawkes, Burton Watson, John Minford, Stephen Owen and others. It is noticeable that these English and American sinologists were soon joined by Chinese scholars residing in the West, such as Hongming (Tomson) Gu and Lin Yutang, among others. They took up the job because they thought it was their obligation to give English readers more faithful translations than Western sinologists could, who, as their target language is their mother tongue, often misinterpret the original text and misrepresent Chinese culture. Since the 1950s, there has been an increasingly powerful trend for Mainland Chinese translators to render or re-render Chinese classics into foreign languages, English in particular. In our time, this work is gathering momentum, enthusiastically advocated and actively practiced by such well-known translation experts as Yang Xianyi of Beijing Foreign Language Press, Xu Yuanchong of Beijing University, Wang Rongpei of Dalian Foreign Language Institute, Wang Hongyin of Nankai University, Wang Hong of Soochow University, Li Zhengshuan of Hebei Normal University, and many more. These professors are not just translators, but also scholars in translation studies. More importantly, some of them, Xu Yuanchong, Wang Hong and Li Zhengshuan, for example, have had their translations published by Western publishers, which suggests that their English meets the international standard.

In the case of our project, we request that the translators do their best to produce good translations. When they submit them to us, they should represent the highest level that they can attain. Then the general editors appointed by the School read the translated texts and remove inaccurate renderings and grammar mistakes if there are any. On top of that, we've taken an indispensable measure to ensure that our English is readable. We asked Ms. Joan Cecile Boulerice, an American teacher who has been teaching English in our school since 2009, to read every text that we've translated and improve the English by making it more natural and idiomatic. This is the best we can do. Of course any problems that still remain in the translations are ours. They have nothing to do with our American teacher.

As the project is well under way, we would like to thank all those who have helped to make it possible. Ms Guo Muyu, director of the South and Southeast Asia Editorial Department, Yunnan People's Publishing House, has been most helpful in our cooperation. In addition, she has added importance to the project by turning it into a national publication project. Yunnan Normal University has supported us by paying the publication fees so that the translators won't have to be burdened with the financial responsibilities for this project. Professor Li Zhengshuan and Professor Wang Hong not only have always encouraged us to go on but have also written the forewords for the project, putting it in a global perspective. Ms Joan Boulerice's revision has ensured the fluency of the translated texts. Finally, special thanks must be given to Professor Wang Hong, again, and Mr Li Lin of Hunan People's Press for their suggestion that has helped us conceive the project from the very beginning.

(The General Editors, School of Foreign Languages & Literature, Yunnan Normal University, Kunming)

十二奴局 // Twelve Nujus

A Brief Introduction to *Twelve Nujus*

Twelve Nujus is a multi-part ballad of the Hani ethnic group, who mostly reside in the mountainous areas between the Red River and the Mekong River in southern Yunnan Province. Nuju is a Hani word, meaning ancient songs, or tunes. So *Twelve Nujus* means "twelve ancient songs". In narrative form, these songs cover important themes like the creation of the world, group history, agricultural production, ethics and morals, ceremonies and festivals. For the Hani people who didn't have their own written language for a long time, these songs served to preserve and pass on their knowledge and values, and at the same time united and inspired the Hani community through hard times.

As an intrinsic part of the Hani people's life, these songs are usually sung with no accompaniment, by well-respected singers known as Mopi. They are sung at significant events like weddings, funerals, festivals and banquets. Dependent on the occasion, the singer might choose one or more Nujus to present. As singers generally sing from memory with poetic license during the performance, the wording might vary slightly each time, or among different singers. That explains why *Twelve Nujus* has a few alternate versions.

In an effort to preserve the oral tradition of the Hani culture, some versions have been recorded and transcribed in recent years. The current translation takes the version of Zhao Guanlu et al. (2009) by Yunnan People's Publishing House as the source text.

The Translator

目录

十二奴局

牡底密底 // 1

牡普谜帕 // 13

昂煞息思 // 29

阿资资斗 // 45

阿扎多拉 // 57

阿匹松阿 // 73

觉麻普德 // 93

牡实米戛 // 111

杜达纳嘎 // 117

汪咀达玛 // 155

觉车里祖 // 167

伙及拉及 // 183

Twelve Nujus / Contents

Mudimidi // 1

Mupumipa // 13

Angshaxisi // 29

Azizidou // 45

Azhaduola // 57

Apisong'a // 73

Juema Pude // 93

Mushimiga // 111

Duda'naga // 117

Wangzuidama // 155

Jueche Lizu // 167

Huojilaji // 183

牡底密底
Mudimidi*

---

* 牡底密底：哈尼语，即开天辟地的意思。
Mudimidi means the creation of the world.

十二奴局 // Twelve Nujus

萨啦阿依 ①——
很古很古的时候,
天地混沌不分,
世间没有宽宽的大地,
世间没有高高的蓝天,
天神没有地方住,
地神没有地方住。

世间没有宽宽的大地,
世间没有高高的蓝天,
天神不会在,
四面八方到处走;
地神不会在,
四面八方到处游。

人种不会生出来,
财种不会生出来,
庄稼不会长出来,
万物不会生出来,
不造天不行了,

Sala Ayi ①–
It was a very long time ago,
When the world was a blur.
The broad earth had its bounds unclear,
And the high blue sky was yet to appear.
Heavenly gods were roaming about,
And earthly ones were unsettled.

The broad earth had its bounds unclear
And the high blue sky was yet to appear;
Heavenly gods had nowhere to stay,
But just wandered about;
Earthly gods had nowhere to stay,
But just roamed in and out.

It was impossible for humans to appear;
It was impossible for fortune to appear;
It was impossible for crops to grow;
It was impossible for everything to grow.
The sky had to be created;

---

① 萨啦阿依:哈尼诗歌演唱起首的衬词。

① Typical opening line in Hani songs and folklore

牡底密底
Mudimidi

不造地不行了。	The earth had to be created.
天是哪日造的？	On what day was the sky made?
地是哪天造的？	On what day was the earth created?
天是属龙的那天造的，	The Day of the Dragon saw the sky's birth,
地是属蛇的那天造的。	And the Day of the Snake, that of the earth.
造天的是哪个？	Who was the one to make the sky?
造地的是哪个？	Who was the one to create the earth?
造天的是朱比阿龙①，	Zhubi Along① made the sky,
造地的是朱比拉沙②。	And Zhubi Lasha② created the earth.
天是怎样造的？	How was the sky made?
地是怎样造的？	How was the earth created?
阿龙把天一片一片辟出来，	Bit by bit Along carved the sky out.
拉沙把地一块一块开出来。	Piece by piece Lasha chipped the earth out.
天劈出来了，	Now the sky was made,
地开出来了，	And the earth created.
可是劈出来的天，	But the carved sky was rough,
高高低低不整齐，	With its surface rising and falling,

---

① 朱比阿龙：哈尼族传说中造天的神。
② 朱比拉沙：哈尼族传说中造地的神。

① Zhubi Along: the Hani god who created the sky.
② Zhubi Lasha: the Hani god who created the earth.

十二奴局 // Twelve Nujus

可是开出来的地，	And the chipped earth bumpy,
坑坑洼洼不平坦。	Pitted with holes here and there.
轮着耙天啰，	It's time to rake the sky level;
轮着耙地啰。	It's time to rake the earth flat.
借来天神的金耙，	Golden rakes and oxen were borrowed
借来天神的黄牛，	From the heavenly gods;
天头耙三道，	After three strikes in the front,
天中耙三道，	Three strikes in the middle,
天脚耙三道，	And three strikes in the end,
把天耙平了。	The sky was raked level.
借来天神的银耙，	Silver rakes and buffalos were borrowed
借来天神的水牛，	From the heavenly gods;
地头耙三道，	After three strikes in the front,
地中耙三道，	Three strikes in the middle,
地脚耙三道，	And three strikes in the end,
把地耙平了。	The earth was raked flat.
天的四方平滑了，	Now the sky turned smooth,
地的四方平坦了，	And the earth even;
可是天和地空空荡荡，	But the space between the two
到处是漆黑一团。	Was just filled with dark void.

牡底密底
Mudimidi

他们用金子做成太阳，	They created the sun with gold,
用玉石做成月亮，	The moon with jade,
用银子做成星星，	And the stars with silver;
挂在高高的天上；	All were hung high in the sky,
从此天上有光亮了，	Brightening the sky,
从此地上有光亮了。	Illuminating the earth.

莫米① 用木梳把太阳光梳下来，　　Momi① combed the sun and the moon,
莫米用木梳把月亮光梳下来。　　　Brushing down threads of lights.
太阳撒下十二道金线，　　　　　　Twelve golden threads were from the Sun,
月亮撒下十二道银线：　　　　　　And twelve silver threads from the moon:
一条线照天边，　　　　　　　　　One thread was cast upon the sky's corner,
一条线照地边，　　　　　　　　　One upon the earth's edge,
一条线照天和地中间，　　　　　　One upon the air in between,
一条线照人，　　　　　　　　　　One upon human beings,
一条线照飞禽，　　　　　　　　　One upon the birds,
一条线照走兽，　　　　　　　　　One upon the beasts,
一条线照河流，　　　　　　　　　One upon the rivers,
一条线照山冈，　　　　　　　　　One upon the low hills,
一条线照长谷子的水田，　　　　　One upon the rice-cultivating paddies,
一条线照长草木的大地，　　　　　One upon the plants thriving lands,
一条线照栽棉花的河坝，　　　　　One upon the cotton growing river dams,

---

① 莫米：哈尼族传说中的天神。　　① The ruling god in Hani legend.

十二奴局 // Twelve Nujus

一条线照栽荞子的高山。	One upon the buckwheat farming high mountains.
四面八方都照到了，	Every corner was illuminated
世间没有照不着的地方了。	With no single place left in the dark.

云雾是怎样来的？	How did the clouds come into being?
山风是怎样来的？	How did the wind take shape?
天上的雷声是怎样来的？	How did the lightning take place?
天边的闪电是怎样来的？	How was the thunder formed?

天上的俄求① 想霸占地，	Eqiu① from the sky coveted the earth;
地上的卑甲阿玛② 想霸占天，	Beijia'ama② from the earth wanted the sky.
两个互不相让，	Neither of them would yield,
拿起大刀争斗起来。	But just picked up their swords
从地上打到天上，	Fighting from the earth to the sky,
从天上打到地上。	And from the sky to the earth.

俄求呼出来的气成云雾，	Eqiu's breath turned into clouds,
卑甲阿玛呼出来的气成山风。	And Beijia'ama's into wind.
它们的吼声变成雷鸣，	Thunder came as the two roared,
它们的汗水变成雨点，	And raindrops fell as they sweated.
它们的刀碰在一处，	As their swords clashed,
冒出的火星变成闪电。	The flying sparks became lightning.

---

① 俄求：传说是龙的别种。
② 卑甲阿玛：传说中的一种动物。

① A legendary dragon-like animal in Hani tradition.
② A legendary animal in Hani tradition.

牡底密底
Mudimidi

最初人种是从哪里来？
长得像个什么样？
男的名字叫什么？
女的名字叫哪样？

最初的时候，
莫米从天上派下两个人种来，
男的叫依沙然哈①，
女的叫依莫然玛②，
只有一只独眼，
长在脑门正中间，
依沙和依莫结成夫妻，
生下一个葫芦团。
过了七天七夜，
葫芦里响起声音；
刚把葫芦划开，
跳出很多人来，
仔细数数看看，
共有七十七种人……

From where did human species come?
What did the first humans look like?
What was the name of the first man?
What was the name of the first woman?

In the very beginning,
Momi sent two humans from the sky,
With the man named Yisha Ranha①,
And the woman Yimo Ranma②.
They each had just one eye,
Right in the middle of their forehead.
Yisha and Yimo became a married couple,
Before giving birth to a gourd-shaped ball.
Seven days and nights had passed by,
And voices were heard from inside.
As the gourd was cut open,
Out jumped a crowd of people,
Who by a thorough count,
Were of seventy-seven races…

① 伊沙然哈：哈尼族传说中白人，沙是名字，然哈即……传说中白人……名字，然玛即

① Yisha Ranha: the earliest man in Hani legend. Yisha is his name and Ranha means "man".
② Yimo Ranma: the earliest woman in Hani legend. Yimo is her name and Ranma means "woman".

十二奴局 // Twelve Nujus

七十七种人生成一副模样，	Seventy seven races of people were all alike,
一个也不像依沙依莫，	Bearing no likeness to Yisha or Yimo;
一只大大的独眼睛，	Each had one big eye,
长在后脑壳上。	In the back of the head.
眼睛在一边，	With the single eye facing one side,
脚手在一边，	And four limbs facing the other,
要倒着走路，	People had to walk backward,
做起活来像扯羊肚肠。	And did their jobs awkwardly.
莫米看到这种人，	At the sight of these people,
他的心一点也不来[①]；	Momi was not happy at all.
要换人种啰，	This species had to be replaced
要生新的一代啰。	By a brand new generation.
后脑独眼一代死了，	The single-eyed generation died,
换了一代新人种。	And a new one appeared.
这代新人种，	The newly born species
长着两只眼睛了。	Had a pair of eyes now.
可是这两只眼睛，	But the eyes were misplaced,
分开长在两个膝头上。	Each located on one knee.
只顾脚不顾手，	So their legs were guided but their arms not,

---

① "心不来"即不喜欢的意思。

做起活来东倒西歪。	And people were clumsy doing their jobs.
莫米看到这种人，	At the sight of these people,
他的心一点也不来；	Momi was not happy at all.
要换人种啰，	This species had to be replaced
要生新的一代啰。	By a brand new generation.
莫米心不来，	Momi stayed dissatisfied,
人种换了一代又一代。	As new species kept replacing old ones.
不知过了多少年，	It was only after countless years,
又生出新的人一代。	When a novel generation came along.
这代人的眼睛有两只，	People of this time had two eyes,
齐齐地长在鼻子边上。	Aligned above the nose;
长得和现在的人一个样，	Just like the people we see now,
做起活来也方便。	They did their jobs with great ease.
莫米看到这代人，	At the sight of these people,
心头老实喜欢。	Momi was more than pleased.
从此不再换人种，	No more replacement was needed,
叫人代代照着这代人样生。	And people could just pass on this species.
从此不知过了多少年，	From then on, whatever the year,
不知过了多少代，	Whatever the generation,
不论到天边，	Whether at the end of the earth,
不论到海边，	Or at the edge of the sea,

不论到哪里，	Wherever it is,
世间人都是一个样，	People of this world would be all alike,
两只眼睛长在鼻子上边。	With two eyes aligned above the nose.
最初的兽种怎样来？	How did the first beast come to life?
最初的鸟种怎样来？	How did the first bird take form?
撒兽种的是哪个？	Who spread the seeds of the beast?
撒鸟种的是哪个？	Who cast the seeds of the bird?
依沙然哈撒兽种，	Yisha Ranha spread the seeds of the beast;
依莫然玛撒鸟种。	Yimo Ranma cast the seeds of the bird.
依沙然哈把兽种撒在地上，	Yisha Ranha spread the beast seeds on the ground,
兽种很快变成螃蟹。	Which were transformed into crabs.
螃蟹进水抱蛋，	In the water the crabs hatched eggs
抱出七十七种走兽……	And out came seventy-seven kinds of beasts…
依莫然玛把鸟种撒到天上，	Yimo Ranma cast the bird seeds across the sky,
鸟种很快变成蝙蝠。	Which were transformed into bats.
大风把蝙蝠吹碎，	A gale torn the bats into pieces,
变成七十七种飞鸟……	Which turned into seventy-seven kinds of birds…
最初草种怎样来？	Where were the first grass seeds from?
最初树种怎样来？	Where were the first tree seeds from?
撒草种的是哪个？	Who scattered the grass seeds?

牡底密底
Mudimidi

撒树种的是哪个？	Who scattered the tree seeds?

依沙然哈撒下草种， Yisha Ranha scattered the grass seeds,
依莫然玛撒下树种。 And Yimo Ranma scattered the tree seeds.
草种很快长成谷子， The grass seeds soon developed into millet,
一颗谷子像拳头一样； A grain of which was as big as a fist;
马蹄踏碎谷子， Smashed by the tramping hoofs,
变成七十七种粮食…… They turned into seventy-seven kinds of crops…
树种很快长成大树， The tree seeds soon grew into tall trees,
一个果子像磨盘一样； Bearing fruits as big as millstones.
鸟雀啄破果子， Pecking birds cracked the fruits.
变成七十七种树木…… Out came seventy-seven kinds of trees.

哈木① 把地界划出来， Hamu① set the land boundaries,
戛卡② 把大路辟出来， Gaka② carved out the roads,
欧卡③ 把水沟开出来， Ouka③ opened up the ditches,
螃蟹把水分出来， Crabs set the water apart,
鸭子把水引出来， Before ducks drew it out.
喝泽美膀④ 把田造出来， Hezemeibang④ created the crop fields;
阿妣仰遮⑤ 把寨子建起来， Apiyangzhe⑤ built up the villages

---

① 哈木：哈尼语，即鹌鹑。
② 戛卡：一种动物。
③ 欧卡：一种动物。
④ 喝泽美膀：一种动物。
⑤ 阿妣仰遮：传说中建寨的始祖。

① Hamu: the Hani word for quail.
② Gaka: a legendary animal.
③ A legendary animal.
④ A legendary animal.
⑤ The Hani ancestor who built villages.

欧巴、欧牛①把寨名取出来，	Which were named by Oba and Oniu①;
遮依遮车②把水井挖出来，	Wells were dug out by Zheyizheche②,
欧比吉莫、龙冲牛斗③把水井管起来，	Of which Oubijimo and Longchongniudou③ were put in charge.
可阿、可遮④把房子盖起来，	Ke'a and Kezhe④ built the houses,
收洛阿秋⑤把火种燃起来……	And Shouluo'aqiu⑤ kindled the fire...
天有了，	Hence the sky was set,
地有了，	And the earth established.
天上样样都有了，	The sky was short of nothing,
一样东西也不差；	With no single item left out;
地上万物都有了，	The earth was short of nothing,
一样东西也不少。	With no single item left out;
天神住在天上高兴了，	The heavenly gods were happily settled in the sky,
地神住在地上喜欢了。	And the earthly gods were contented where they were.
众：萨—萨⑥！	Chorus: Sah-Sah!⑥

---

① 欧巴、欧牛：传说中取寨名的始祖。
② 遮依遮车：传说中建水井的始祖。
③ 欧比吉莫、龙冲牛斗：传说中管水的始祖。
④ 可阿、可遮：传说中盖房子的始祖。
⑤ 收洛阿秋：传说中播火种的始祖。
⑥ 哈尼族歌手演唱完一节或一段诗歌后听众的附和声。

① The two Hani ancestors who named the villages.
② The Hani ancestor who dug wells.
③ The two Hani ancestors who were in charge of water supply.
④ The two Hani ancestors who built houses.
⑤ The Hani ancestor who kept the fire.
⑥ Typical response made by audiences at the end of a song.

牡普谜帕
Mupumipa*

---

* 牡普谜帕：哈尼语，即天翻地覆的意思。
  Mupumipa means the sky and the earth turned upside down.

十二奴局 // Twelve Nujus

萨啦阿依——	Sala Ayi–
天风从天上吹下来，	The heavenly winds blew from the sky,
地风从地下冒出来；	And the earthly winds from the earth.
天风呼啦啦离地三脚掌，	The heavenly winds howled three soles above the earth,
地风呼啦啦离天三巴掌。	And the earthly winds roared three palms below the sky.
天风和地风碰在一起，	The two gusts of winds twisted,
天地摇晃着轰隆作响。	Rocking the sky and the earth loudly.
天地之间没有柱子撑持，	With no pillars in between,
天塌下来了，	The sky was falling down,
地翻上来了，	And the earth turned up.
洪水淹没大地，	The flood came to inundate
洪水淹到天上，	Both the earth and the sky,
分不清天边地边在哪里。	Blurring the bounds between the two.
大人淹死完了，	All adults were drowned to death;
小娃淹死完了；	All children were drowned to death;
男人淹死完了，	All men were drowned to death;
女人淹死完了。	All women were drowned to death,
世上只剩下莫鲁和沙崩两兄妹，	Except for Molu and his sister Shabeng,
躲在一个大葫芦里漂在洪水上。	Who hid in a big gourd drifting in the flood.

牡普谜帕
Mupumipa

不知过了多少年月，	Countless years had passed
洪水渐渐退下去。	Before the waters receded.
大水退到哪里，	Wherever the flood went,
葫芦也漂到哪里。	The gourd drifted along.
大水退到汪洋大海去了，	As the waters reached the sea,
葫芦却挂在一棵大松树上。	The gourd ended up hung on a big pine tree.
兄妹俩钻出葫芦一看，	The two crawled out of the gourd,
上不沾天下不着地，	Only to find themselves lost.
头上是云雾翻滚，	Storm clouds were rolling above,
脚下是万丈深渊。	While the bottomless abyss was lying below.
哥哥愁得皱眉头，	The brother frowned at the sight,
妹妹气得淌眼泪。	And the sister was all tears in despair.
高高的松树上，	High up on the pine tree,
老鹰筑有窝，	There was an eagle nest.
窝里三只小鹰叫，	Three eaglets were chirping,
探头张嘴等待老鹰来喂食。	Neck-stretched waiting to be fed.
一条毒蛇爬上树，	A venomous snake slithered up the tree,
吐着分杈的长舌头，	Flicking its forked tongue out,
倏倏扑向老鹰窝。	And approached the nest hissing.
小鹰要飞飞不起，	The baby eagles tried to fly but in vain;
小鹰要跳跳不动。	They tried to jump but failed.

三只小鹰被吓坏，	Terrified and desperate,
可可怜怜挤作一团，	They huddled together in misery,
吱吱地哭叫喊爹妈。	Squawking for their parents' help.
兄妹俩看见心着急，	The two people were worried at the sight,
想好主意爬到树梢，	But soon came up with an idea.
各人劈下一根松枝，	Each climbed up to cut off a tree branch,
奋力把毒蛇打死。	With which they strived to kill the snake.
他们将毒蛇掐断，	They cut the snake into pieces,
一截一截给鹰儿喂食。	And fed the eaglets one by one.
大老鹰寻食回来了，	The eagle parents came back from hunting,
三只小鹰忙告诉爹妈：	And the babies hurried to tell:
"我们已经吃了一顿最好的饭菜，	"We've had the best meal ever.
肚子饱鼓鼓，	Now our bellies are full,
什么也吃不得了。"	With no room for anything at all."
老鹰听了感到奇怪，	The eagles felt surprised at the words,
就细细盘问小鹰：	And sought details from their kids:
"是谁好心喂你们，	"Who was so nice to feed you?
孩儿都吃了些什么饭菜？"	And what did you have for your meal?"
三只小鹰像芋头冒芽，	Like taro sprouting shoots,
争着告诉爹妈：	The three eaglets vied to talk:
"爹妈出窝去寻食，	"When you were out hunting for food,

牡普谜帕
Mupumipa

有条毒蛇来吃我们，	A vicious snake approached to eat us;
是他们兄妹来救命，	Two people came to our rescue,
打死毒蛇掐断蛇肉喂饱我们。"	Killing the snake and feeding us with its meat."

老鹰听了心里感激，　　　　The eagle parents were very thankful,
扇着翅膀感谢兄妹俩：　　　Flapping their wings to express their gratitude:
"你们是心肠最好的人，　　"You are the nicest people in the world,
怪不得世间只剩你们；　　　No wonder you could survive.
你们搭救了我们的孩子，　　You have saved our children,
我们想法送你们到地上。"　In return we will send you to the ground."

兄妹俩担心老鹰背不动，　　Doubtful about the eagles' strength,
互相望望不出声气。　　　　The two looked at each other saying nothing.
公老鹰猜透了他们的心理，　The male eagle, reading their minds,
张开翅膀飞到了地上。　　　Spread his wings and flew down.
一只翅膀背上一扇磨，　　　Carrying one millstone on each wing,
稳稳当当地飞回到松树上。　He flew back steadily to the pine tree.
然后又把两扇磨，　　　　　Then he returned the millstones
轻轻送回到地上。　　　　　Lightly back to the ground.

兄妹俩见了好欢喜，　　　　The two people were thrilled,
一股暖流涌上心房。　　　　Feeling warm in their hearts.
他们对老鹰点头，　　　　　They nodded at the eagles,
他们向老鹰招手。　　　　　Waving their hands to them.

十二奴局 // Twelve Nujus

公老鹰张开翅膀，	The male eagle unfolded his wings,
把哥哥莫鲁背下地，	Carrying Molu down to the ground;
母老鹰张开翅膀，	The female eagle spread her wings,
把妹妹沙崩背到地上。	Taking Shabeng down to the ground.

兄妹俩到了地上，	Upon arrival on the ground,
哥哥对妹妹讲：	The brother told his sister:
"你到东边找一找，	"Would you look in the east
看看还有没有挖田的男人；	For men that can plow the field?
我到西边看一看，	I will search in the west
瞧瞧还有没有砍柴的姑娘。"	For girls who can cut wood."

哥哥往西边去了，	The brother went westward,
妹妹朝东边走了。	And the sister eastward.
九座山跑遍不见一个脚迹，	But no single footprint was traced in nine hills,
九条冲走遍听不到一样声音。	And no single voice was heard in nine valleys.
他们找遍东南西北，	They tried all directions,
四面八方没有一个人影。	But failed to find a single person.
不知找了多少天，	Infinite days of searching had passed,
每天只是两兄妹遇在一起。	And the two found no one but each other.

世上没有其他女人哟，	With no other woman in this world,
哥哥莫鲁找不着妻子；	Molu could not find a wife;
世上没有其他男人哟，	With no other man in the world,

牡普谜帕
Mupumipa

妹妹沙崩找不着丈夫。	Shabeng could not find a husband.
眼看世间快要绝人种，	Seeing the prospect of human extinction,
想到宽宽大地缺主人，	Unable to find masters for the broad earth,
哥哥急得像老水牛喘粗气，	The brother sighed like a buffalo,
妹妹气得淌眼泪。	And the sister shed tears of sadness.

一个天气晴朗的日子，	On a bright sunny day,
兄妹俩来到一条河边。	The two came to a riverside.
哥哥对妹妹说：	The brother told his sister,
"活着的人一处也找不着，	"With no people living around,
我们两兄妹难生活了，	It'll be hard for us to survive.
用树叶测测看吧，	Let's trust our fortune in the leaves,
也许它们能告诉我们怎么办。"	Which may tell us what to do."

哥哥先摘一片水冬瓜叶子，	The brother picked a leaf of winter melon,
轻轻丢进河水里；	And dropped it gently into the river.
妹妹也摘一片水冬瓜叶子，	The sister picked a leaf as well,
跟着哥哥丢进河水里。	And dropped it into the water.

两片叶子翻上翻下漂，	The two leaves floated up and down,
顺着河水淌下去。	Drifting down the river.
哥哥追着树叶跑，	Both the brother and the sister
妹妹追着树叶跑，	Chased the leaves running.
叶子淌到河尾沙滩上，	Reaching the beach downstream,

十二奴局 // Twelve Nujus

两片叶子合拢沾在一起了：　　The two leaves folded together,
哥哥的叶子在上面，　　　　　With the brother's on top
妹妹的叶子在下面。　　　　　And the sister's down below.

一个天气暖和的日子，　　　　On a warm and cozy day,
兄妹俩来到一座高山上。　　　The two came to a high mountain.
妹妹对哥哥说：　　　　　　　The sister told her brother,
"世上没有活着的人了，　　　 "With no living people around,
我们不会生活下去，　　　　　It's unlikely for us to survive.
滚石头测测看吧，　　　　　　Let's trust our fate with rolling stones,
也许石头会告诉我们怎么办。" Which might tell us what to follow."

妹妹拣了一块石头，　　　　　The sister picked up a stone,
哥哥拣了一块石头，　　　　　And the brother followed suit.
妹妹先把石头滚下山，　　　　The sister threw the stone down the hill,
哥哥也跟着把石头滚下山。　　And the brother did the same as well.

两块石头翻着跟斗滚下去了，Two stones rolled down the hill,
兄妹俩跟着跑下山去看石头。And the two people followed running.
石头滚到山脚，　　　　　　　At the bottom of the hill,
两块石头合拢摞在一起：　　　The two stones were stacked,
哥哥的石头在上面，　　　　　With the brother's on top,
妹妹的石头在下面。　　　　　And the sister's down below.

牡普谜帕
Mupumipa

妹妹看见石头,	Seeing the stacked stones,
羞红的脸像一朵花,	The sister blushed like a rose,
转过背去不说话;	And turned away saying nothing.
哥哥看见石头,	Seeing the stacked stones,
红着脸对妹妹说:	The brother told his sister blushing,
"亲亲的阿妹哟,	"My beloved sister,
树叶子测过了,	We've sought answers from the leaves;
石头也测过了,	We've sought answers from the stones.
放河水漂的树叶,	The leaves drifting along the river
最后是贴在一起;	Ended up folded together;
从山上滚下去的石头,	The stones rolling down the hill
最后是摞在一起。	Ended up stacked together.
不想见也见着了,	Like it or not,
想见也见着了,	We see what we see.
世上活着的只有我们兄妹,	As the only two living in this world,
我们到底该怎么办?"	What are we supposed to do?"
妹妹低着头,	With lowered head,
像蚊子哼一样细声:	The sister spoke with a voice like a mosquito,
"问问莫托库鲁舍①,	"Let's ask Motuokulushe①,
他咋个说就咋个办。"	And take whatever advice he gives."

---

① 莫托库鲁舍:传说中的天神之一。

① One of the heavenly gods.

兄妹俩对着苍天叩头，	The two kowtowed to the sky,
齐声向苍天呼喊：	Before shouting in chorus:
"仁慈的莫托库鲁舍啊，	"Merciful Motuokulushe,
洪水滔天人间受灾难，	After the disastrous flood,
世上的人都死完了，	All the people are dead,
只剩下我们兄妹了。	Except the two of us.
求你不要让世间绝人种，	To keep the human race alive,
给我们指永生的路吧！"	Would you please show us the way out?"

天空忽然闪现一道金光，	A golden light flashed across the sky,
同时传来一个声音：	Accompanied by a voice:
"世间数你们兄妹俩心最好，	"You two are the most kind-hearted,
我特意把你们留下。	And that's why I kept you alive.
你们兄妹成一家，	You two can get married;
你们兄妹做夫妻，	You two can start a family.
男耕女织传人种，	The man farms and the woman weaves,
一代一代人会兴旺。"	Then the human race will survive and prosper."

哥哥听了对妹妹说：	The brother spoke to his sister,
"亲亲的阿妹哟，	"My beloved sister,
莫托库鲁舍的话你听见了，	You heard Motuokulushe.
为了传人种，	To keep the human race from dying out,
我们就做夫妻吧。"	Let's become husband and wife."

牡普谜帕
Mupumipa

妹妹用手蒙着脸说：	The sister said covering her face,
"亲亲的阿哥，	"My beloved brother,
害羞也顾不得了，	Shame and shyness put aside,
就听莫托库鲁舍的话，	Let's take Motuokulushe's advice
我们就做一家吧。"	And get settled as a couple."
兄妹俩成了一家，	The two became husband and wife;
兄妹俩做了夫妻，	The two got settled as a couple.
为了传人种，	To pass the human race on,
辛辛苦苦生儿育女。	They worked hard raising children.
他们生了三个儿子，	They gave birth to three sons
他们生了三个姑娘。	As well as three daughters.
儿子姑娘一天天长大了，	Day by day as the boys and girls grew up,
莫鲁和沙崩心里像装了一缸蜜糖。	Molu and Shabeng were filled with honey-like happiness.
一把荞子绿一片，	A handful of buckwheat spreads the green,
一股龙潭水润一方，	While the gush of the wellspring wets an area.
为了快快繁衍人类，	To multiply the human race fast,
他们把儿女打发到四面八方。	They would send their children to all directions.
听说要到别的地方，	Hearing the parents' plan,
大儿子心里老实欢喜：	The oldest son was full of joy:
"亲亲的阿爸阿妈，	"My beloved dad and mom,

我人大脚杆粗，	As the oldest and the strongest,
让我到高山上去吧，	I'd like to go to the hilltops,
两个弟弟留在平坝。"	Leaving my brothers to the flatland."

听说大哥要到高山去，	Learning about his brother's plan,
二儿子也说出了自己的想法：	The middle son spoke his mind,
"亲亲的阿爸阿妈，	"My dear mom and dad,
我的腿力好，	I got strong feet,
让我到半山去吧，	So I'd like to go to the hillside,
留下弟弟在平坝。"	Leaving my youngest brother in the flatland."

三儿子听了哥哥们的话，	Hearing all of these words,
心里有些气不平：	The youngest son couldn't stay calm:
"阿爸和阿妈，	"My dear mom and dad,
我人小会长大，	Young for now, I will grow up one day.
让我和哥哥们在一起，	I want to be with my brothers,
相亲相爱不分离。"	Staying near and dear forever."

莫鲁和沙崩开导儿子：	Molu and Shabeng reasoned,
"我的儿哟，	"My dear sons,
传人种是天神的意旨，	It's the god's will to pass our race on.
不能为了弟兄的情意，	Don't let your love for each other
耽误了人间的大事。	Ruin this biggest mission in the world.
你们同是一个父母养，	Born and raised up in this family,

牡普谜帕
Mupumipa

大家同是一个父母生，	You are equally cherished,
手心手背都是肉，	And bonded to us the way
树枝树叶连着根；	Branches and leaves are to the root.
不管到天头地脚，	No matter how faraway you go,
永远是亲亲的一家弟兄。"	You'll be dear to each other forever."

一家人商量好了，　　　　　Thus an agreement was reached,
弟兄们要分开了，　　　　　And the brothers were set to part.
莫鲁和沙崩心里高兴，　　　Molu and Shabeng were delighted
把道理讲给儿女们听：　　　Telling their children something important:
"大水淹没人世的时候，　　"When the waters flooded the world,
多亏纳米堵合①的青松将我们　A pine tree on Namiduhe① saved our lives.
　　搭救，　　　　　　　　No matter where you go,
孩儿不管到了什么地方，　　You should always honor pine trees."
遇到松树要磕头拜礼。

"每年过节的日子，　　　　"On New Year's Day every year,
要把青松接来家里，　　　　You should take pine trees to your home,
要给它烧香磕头，　　　　　Burn incense sticks, and kowtow to them,
还要用酒肉饭菜献祭。"　　Offering them a sacrifice of meat and wine."

大儿子大姑娘配一对，　　　The oldest son and daughter were married,

---

① 纳米堵合：哈尼语，一座高山。　　① A high mountain.

十二奴局 // Twelve Nujus

到高山安家去了；
二儿子二姑娘配一对，
到半山腰安家去了；
三儿子三姑娘配一对，
到平地安家去了。

火苗亮闪闪，
烟火冲上天，
人间又有人种了，
莫托库鲁舍看见心欢喜。

为了让人种一代一代传下去，
为了让人类一代一代快发展，
不能让天再坍下来，
不能让地再翻过来；
要把天锁起来，
要把地锁起来。

莫托库鲁舍想出办法，
派来阿朗、阿汪① 两位神主，
在天和地中间立柱子，
把天撑起来，

---

① 阿朗、阿汪：哈尼传说中锁天锁地的神。

Who went to settle on the hilltop;
The middle son and daughter were married,
Who went to settle on the hillside;
The youngest son and daughter were married,
Who went to settle on the flatland.

Flames were sparkling on the ground,
While chimney smoke was rising to the sky.
Seeing the human race spread across the earth,
Motuokulushe was filled with joy.

For the human race to expand
From one generation to another,
Never will the sky be allowed to fall,
Nor will the earth turn over again.
The sky was to be chained up,
And the earth to be confined.

Motuokulushe came up with an idea,
Sending Alang and Awang① the two gods,
To set up pillars in the air,
Which held up the sky,

---

① The two gods who locked the sky and the earth in Hani legend.

牡普谜帕
Mupumipa

把地压下来，	And pressed down the earth.
用锁把天锁起来，	With locks the sky was chained up;
用锁把地锁起来。	With locks the earth was confined.

阿朗拿来天神的柱子，　　Alang brought the gods' pillars,
选好立柱子的地基。　　　And chose proper sites.
东边立起金柱子，　　　　Gold pillars were erected in the east,
南边立起银柱子，　　　　Silver ones in the south,
西边立起铜柱子，　　　　Bronze ones in the west,
北边立起铁柱子。　　　　And iron ones in the north.

阿汪拿来天神的大锁，　　Awang brought the gods' huge locks,
把天地的四方锁起来。　　And fastened up the four corners.
东方用金锁锁起来，　　　Gold locks were used in the east,
南方用银锁锁起来，　　　Silver ones in the south,
西方用铜锁锁起来，　　　Bronze ones in the west,
北方用铁锁锁起来。　　　And iron ones in the north.

阿朗立好柱子，　　　　　After setting up the pillars,
向万物发了誓言，　　　　Alang made a vow to all creatures,
打下木刻作记号：　　　　Which was carved onto a block.
大公鸡的冠子上打了刻，　Roosters had their crests branded with the block,
老水牛的角上打了刻，　　And buffalo had their horns branded.
山羊的角上打了刻，　　　Goats had their horns marked,

十二奴局 // Twelve Nujus

蛇的身上打了刻，	Serpents had their trunks marked,
哈尼妇女的包头上打了刻，	And the Hani women had their headscarves marked
从此天不会坍下来。	That the sky would never fall down again.

阿旺锁好锁，	After fastening the locks,
向万物发了誓言，	Awang made a vow to all creatures,
打下木刻作记号：	Which was carved onto a block.
老虎的身上打了刻，	Tigers were branded with the block,
豹子的身上打了刻，	So were the leopards;
彝家女人的衣边上打了刻，	Yi women's clothes were marked,
傣家姑娘的裙子上打了刻，	So were Dai girls' dresses,
汉人妇女的小脚上打了刻，	And the bundled feet of Han women.
从此地不会翻过来。	Thus the earth will never turn over again.

天地中间立起了柱子，	So the pillars were put up in between,
天地锁上了神锁，	While the sky and earth were locked up.
阿朗、阿汪发了誓言，	Alang and Awang made their vows,
阿朗、阿旺打下了刻，	Which were carved onto blocks.
天不会坍下来了，	Never again will the sky fall down
地不会翻过来了。	Nor will the earth turn over.
人种一代一代传下来了，	Thus the human race will last;
人类一代一代发起来了。	Thus the human race will prosper.
众：萨—萨！	Chorus: Sah-Sah!

昂煞息思
Angshaxisi*

---

* 昂煞息思：哈尼语，即杀鱼取种。
  Angshaxisi means getting seeds from the fish.

十二奴局 // Twelve Nujus

萨啦阿依——
自从天翻地覆,
洪水淹没大地,
树木和草淹死了,
留着的树木草种冲走了,
藏着的五谷种子冲走了,
大地一片光秃秃,
草木五谷一样也不长。
世上的人们不会过日子,
祈求莫米给种子。

仁慈的莫米告诉人们:
"树种没被水冲走,
草种没被水冲走,
五谷种子没被水冲走,
都被大鱼吃进肚子里。

"赶快找葛麻,
织张大渔网,
大江大河浪滔滔,
大鱼就在水里藏,
快把大鱼打上来,

Sala Ayi–
When the heaven and earth were overturned,
The flood overwhelmed the land.
Trees and grass were drowned to death,
And their seeds flushed away,
Along with the well-kept grain seeds.
On the bleak and barren land,
There was no grass or grain growing.
At a loss for how to survive,
People prayed to Momi for seeds.

Merciful Momi told the people:
"The tree seeds had not been flushed away.
The grass seeds had not been flushed away.
The grain seeds had not been flushed away.
A big fish swallowed them into its belly.

"Go look for some kudzu vines,
With which you'll weave a huge fishing net.
Where the waves are surging,
Is the big fish's hideout.
Haul in the fish with the net,

昂煞息思
Angshaxisi

杀死大鱼取回种。"	Kill it and you will get back the seeds."
不知葛根长在哪里？	Where were kudzu vines rooted?
不知葛根窜在什么地方？	Where did they stretch to?
比出阿玛玛学①去问野猪，	Bichu'amamaxue① went to the wild boar,
好心肠的野猪说：	Who was good-hearted enough to say,
"葛根深深埋地下，	"Kudzu is rooted deep underground,
葛根窜到大河边。"	With vines spreading far into the big river."
九个姑娘去寻葛根藤，	Nine girls set out to find kudzu vines,
倒钩刺把衣裳撕成碎片。	Their clothes were torn into pieces by barbs.
走了三天路，	After three days' walking,
翻过九座山，	When nine mountains were conquered,
大河边上绿汪汪，	The girls came across a lush area of kudzu vines,
到处是老水牛拉不断的葛藤。	Too tough to be pulled apart even by old buffalo.
九个姑娘九把刀哟，	The nine girls, with nine knives,
大河边上采葛藤，	Cut the vines along the big river.
采一根只有一把，	A single vine made only one handful,
割一千根才满一背；	And one thousand, a basket full;
不怕采葛活计苦，	Despite the toil of cutting,
不怕背葛藤腰杆酸疼。	Despite the pain in their backs,
一根一根割出来，	They cut out the vines one by one,

① 传说中最先拿鱼的人。

① The first fisherman in Hani legend.

一背一背背回来。	And shouldered them back basket after basket.
剥下葛藤皮，	They peeled off the bark of the vines,
撕出麻丝纺成线；	And ripped out linen to spin yarn.
纺一根只有一绕，	A piece of twine was made with one vine,
纺完一千根才有一捆。	And a yarn ball, with one thousand.
姑娘剥葛皮从早到晚，	The girls peeled the bark from morning till night,
姑娘纺葛麻从黑夜到天亮。	And spun it from night to daylight.
一根一根葛藤剥下皮，	One by one the vines were stripped;
一捆一捆葛麻纺成线。	One by one the linen spun into pieces of twine.
用线来织网，	The pieces of twine was used for net-weaving,
织几下才是一个眼；	A knot was made after several stitches;
织千眼万眼，	It was only after thousands of knots,
才能织成一张渔网。	That a fishnet could be finally woven.
手指头划破出血不怕，	Despite their bleeding fingers,
手掌心磨出老茧不怕，	Despite their calloused palms,
一眼一眼地织，	They kept weaving one mesh after another,
千眼万眼织出了渔网。	And thousands later the fishing net was done.
十个伙子抬渔网，	Ten young men carried the net,
大河里头撒大鱼；	Fishing in the big river.
织成的渔网撒不开，	The cast net failed to go wide,
漂在水上乱成一团；	But floated on the water messed up.

昂煞息思
Angshaxisi

原来网脚要有铅巴坠，	Obviously lead sinkers were needed,
渔网才会撒开沉入水。	To pull the net deep into the water.

渔网需要铅巴来坠， Lead sinkers were needed,
哪里有铅巴？ But where could the lead be found?
一个认不得， No one knew anything about it,
一个也不有， Or was in possession of any.
要到各个地方赶街子了， People had to go to fairs
去寻找铅巴坠渔网。 In search of lead sinkers for the net.

先去赶羊街， They went to the Sheep Fair first,
羊街街子好热闹， Which was full of hustle and bustle.
赶街人像栽的甘蔗一样密， People crowded like sugarcane in the fields,
喧哗声像打闷雷一样响。 With voices as loud as thunder.

赶街的样样人都有： All walks of life came to the fair:
穿宽袖衣的傣家女人来了， Dai women in wide-sleeved clothes,
戴公鸡帽的彝家姑娘来了， Yi girls wearing rooster-shaped hats,
背秤杆的汉人伙子来了， Han lads with scales on their backs,
会打麂子的瑶家汉子来了， Yao men known as good muntjac hunters.
各种各样的人都来了， All kinds of people came,
四面八方的人都来了。 From far and wide.

转来转去找， They searched and searched,

十二奴局 // Twelve Nujus

转到街头找,	First in the upper street.
街头用的东西样样都有卖,	All things to use were there for sale,
唯独铅巴没人卖。	With the only exception being lead.

转来转去找,　　　　　　　　They searched and searched,
转到街中找,　　　　　　　　Then into the middle street.
街中穿的东西样样都有卖,　　All things to wear were there for sale,
唯独铅巴没人卖。　　　　　　With the only exception being lead.

转来转去找,　　　　　　　　They searched and searched,
转到街尾找,　　　　　　　　Then to the lower street.
街尾吃的东西样样都有卖,　　All things to eat were there for sale,
唯独铅巴没人卖。　　　　　　With the only exception being lead.

买不到铅巴不能回家,　　　　Without lead they couldn't go home,
还要到别处街子去找。　　　　But had to look at other fairs.
赶了羊街赶猪街,　　　　　　The Swine Fair after the Sheep Fair,
赶了猪街赶牛街,　　　　　　Then the Cow Fair was visited;
转到郎特①赶龙街,　　　　　The Dragon Fair in Langte①,
转到阿丕②赶马街,　　　　　The Horse Fair in Api②,
倮玛③鼠街赶过了,　　　　　And the Rat Fair in Luoma③ was searched;

---

① 地名。　　　　　　　　　① A place.
② 地名。　　　　　　　　　② A place.
③ 地名。　　　　　　　　　③ A place.

昂煞息思
Angshaxisi

仰书埕^①街赶过了，	The Fair in Yangshudie①,
托普^②街子赶过了，	The Fair in Tuopu②,
青尼^③街子赶过了。	And the Fair in Qingni③ were all checked.
街上样样东西都有卖，	Everything was there for sale,
唯独铅巴没人卖。	With the only exception being lead.

转来转去看， They searched and searched,
遇着慈戛戈欧姑娘欧巴、欧牛。 Till they met Cigageou's daughter Oba and Ouniu.
问她们见不见有铅巴卖， Asked if they ever saw any lead,
两个姑娘回答说： The two girls replied,
"铅巴这里有， "We have a lead bar ourselves,
铅巴多重要多重的银子来换。" Tradeable for a silver bar of the same weight."

没有铅巴打不着大鱼， Fishing was not possible without lead,
拿出银子买回铅巴。 So they bought the bar readily.
银亮亮的铅巴刺眼睛， The sight of the dazzling lead
男人女人见了心里老实喜欢， Filled the men and women with joy.
请来傣家师傅打网坠， Then a Dai master was asked
铅巴网脚沉甸甸。 To cast heavy sinkers with the lead.

择了最好的日子， On the most auspicious day,
择了最好的时辰， At the most auspicious time,

---

① 地名。 ① A place.
② 地名。 ② A place.
③ 地名。 ③ A place.

抬着大渔网，	People carried the huge net
大河里头打大鱼。	To go fishing in the river.
头回撒下去，	At the first cast,
不见渔网动，	The net stayed still in the water,
只见水泡泡，	Except for some bubbles rising.
没有撒到鱼。	Apparently no fish was caught.
二回撒下去，	At the second cast,
不见渔网动，	The net stayed still in the water.
只见河渣和树叶，	Apart from some mud and leaves,
还是没有撒到鱼。	There were no fish found inside.
三回撒下去，	At the third cast,
渔网不停地动，	The net kept moving,
渔网不停地晃。	The net kept shaking.
十个伙子拉起网，	Ten men hauled in the net
撒着一条大鱼了，	To find a big fish trapped inside,
放在河边沙滩上。	Which was later put on the beach.
鱼头黄得闪金光，	With a glittering yellow head,
鱼尾花得刺眼睛，	A mixed-colored tail,
鱼眼睁得碗样大，	Bowl-sized eyes,
鱼在沙滩上乱蹦乱跳。	The fish was thrashing around.

昂煞息思
Angshaxisi

打着大鱼了，	Now the fish was caught,
寨头的阿波①来看，	Abo① from the upper village,
寨尾的阿皮②来看，	Api② from the lower village,
男女老少都来看，	People of all ages came to see,
谁也说不出是什么鱼。	But all were unable to tell what kind of fish it was.

抬着两拃长的大鱼，　　　　They carried the two-arm-length fish,
四处去问鱼名称。　　　　　Asking around for its name.
抬给罗比③看，　　　　　　Luobi③ had been consulted;
抬给罗梅④看，　　　　　　Luomei④ had been consulted;
抬给布洪⑤看，　　　　　　Buhong⑤ had been consulted;
抬给阿松⑥看……　　　　　Asong⑥ had been consulted...
个个都摇头，　　　　　　　But they all shook their heads,
谁也说不出是什么鱼。　　　Unable to tell what kind of fish it was.

抬着两拃长的大鱼，　　　　They carried the two-arm-length fish,
又到四方问鱼名。　　　　　Asking around for its name.
汉人看过了，　　　　　　　Han people had been turned to;
傣家看过了，　　　　　　　Dai people had been turned to;
彝家看过了，　　　　　　　Yi people had been turned to;

---

① 阿波：即阿爷的意思。
② 阿皮：即阿奶的意思。
③ 罗比：哈尼族支系。
④ 罗梅：哈尼族支系。
⑤ 布洪：哈尼族支系。
⑥ 阿松：哈尼族支系。

---

① The Hani word for grandpa.
② The Hani word for grandma.
③ A branch of the Hani people.
④ A branch of the Hani people.
⑤ A branch of the Hani people.
⑥ A branch of the Hani people

瑶家看过了……	Yao people had been turned to…
个个都摇头，	But they all shook their heads,
一个也认不出是哪样鱼。	Unable to tell what kind of fish it was.
不知是条哪样鱼，	Unable to identify the fish,
人们心里老实着急。	People were truly worried.
对着苍天求莫米，	They prayed to Momi in the heaven,
教教是条哪样鱼。	Begging him to drop some hint.
仁慈的莫米听见了，	Merciful Momi in response,
传下话来给贝玛①：	Passed word to the beima[①]:
"那条大鱼肚里藏珍宝，	"With treasures hidden in its belly,
鱼名只有两个人知道：	The fish had its name known to just two:
一个是阿福根勒阿搓②，	One is Afugenle'acuo[②],
一个是阿车克什也莫阿玛③。"	And the other Achekeshiyeyemo'ama[③]."
人们请来这两个能人，	People consulted these two sages,
才知道这条大鱼叫黄花鱼，	And identified the fish as a yellow croaker.
鱼肚里藏着草木和五谷种子，	Plant and corn seeds were hidden in its belly,
等它闭上眼睛才能拿到。	Accessible only when its eyes were closed.
要杀大鱼取种了，	To kill the fish and take out the seeds,

---

① 贝玛：哈尼族的巫师。
② 哈尼族传说中的善识者。
③ 哈尼族传说中的善识者。

① Hani priests are generally called beima.
② A wise man in Hani culture.
③ A wise man in Hani culture.

昂煞息思
Angshaxisi

先是抬到大江边去杀，	People took the fish to the riverside.
杀了鱼不死，	They tried but the fish stayed alive,
眼睛也不闭。	And its eyes were wide open.
鱼为什么不会死？	Why wouldn't the fish die?
鱼为什么不闭眼？	Why did it keep its eyes open?
因为那里有鲨鱼做伴。	Because sharks were there to keep it company.

又抬到森林里去杀，	People tried to kill the fish in the forest,
杀了鱼不死，	But the fish stayed alive,
眼睛也不闭。	And its eyes were wide open.
鱼为什么不会死？	Why wouldn't the fish die?
鱼为什么不闭眼？	Why did it keep its eyes open?
因为那里是砍柴的地方。	Because that's where wood was chopped.

又抬到田边去杀，	People tried to kill the fish near the fields,
杀了鱼不死，	But failed as the fish stayed alive,
眼睛也不闭。	And its eyes were wide open.
鱼为什么不会死？	Why wouldn't the fish die?
鱼为什么不闭眼？	Why did it keep its eyes open?
因为那里是薅秧丢杂草的地方。	Because that's where weeds were pulled.

又抬到水井边去杀，	People tried to kill the fish near the well,
杀了鱼不死，	But failed as the fish stayed alive,
眼睛也不闭。	And its eyes were wide open.

十二奴局 // Twelve Nujus

鱼为什么不会死？	Why wouldn't the fish die?
鱼为什么不闭眼？	Why did it keep its eyes open?
因为那里是背水的地方。	Because that's where water was fetched.

又抬到猪槽边去杀，
杀了鱼不死，
眼睛也不闭。
鱼为什么不会死？
鱼为什么不闭眼？
因为那里是喂猪食的地方。

People tried to kill the fish near the pig trough,
But failed as the fish stayed alive,
And its eyes were wide open.
Why wouldn't the fish die?
Why did it keep its eyes open?
Because that's where pigs were fed.

又抬到灶门前去杀，
杀了鱼不死，
眼睛也不闭。
鱼为什么不会死？
鱼为什么不闭眼？
因为那里是女人煮饭的地方。

People tried to kill the fish in front of the stove,
But failed as the fish stayed alive,
And its eyes were wide open.
Why wouldn't the fish die?
Why did it keep its eyes open?
Because that's where women cooked.

又抬到哈扎比堵机阿勒①去杀，
鱼不摇头不摆尾，
红彤彤的血淌成河水。
大鱼杀死了，
眼睛闭上了。

People killed it finally in Hazhabiduji'ale,①
Where the fish stopped shaking its body.
Crimson blood gushing out like a river,
The big fish was finally killed,
With its eyes closed forever.

---

① 古地名，不详。

① An ancient place.

昂煞息思
Angshaxisi

这条大鱼肉厚有两拃①，	The big fish was two-palm-length thick,
鱼肚有千层，	With hundreds of fat layers in the belly.
拿着快刀亮闪闪，	With a shiny sharp knife,
一层一层剖鱼肚。	People cut open the belly layer by layer.

剖开第一层鱼肚， When the first layer was cut open,
里面装着三粒谷子。 Three grains of millet were found.
谷子栽在什么地方？ Where to plant the millet?
长杨柳树的龙潭旁。 Beside the pond where the willow trees were growing.

剖开第二层鱼肚， When the second layer was cut open,
里面装着三粒荞子。 Three grains of buckwheat were found.
荞子栽在什么地方？ Where to plant the buckwheat?
长水冬瓜树的山坡上。 On the hillside where the gourd trees were growing.

剖开第三层鱼肚， When the third layer was cut open,
里面装着三粒高粱子。 Three grains of sorghum were found.
高粱栽在什么地方？ Where to plant the sorghum?
长芦苇的山坡上。 On the hillside where the reeds were growing.

剖开第四层鱼肚， When the fourth layer was cut open,
里面装着三粒棉花籽。 Three grains of cotton were found.

---

① 两拃：即一尺。

| 棉花栽在什么地方？ | Where to plant the cotton? |
| 长尖刀草的矮山上。 | On the low hill where the sword grass was growing. |

剖开第五层鱼肚，
里面装着三粒苞谷。
苞谷栽在什么地方？
长锥栗树的山上。

When the fifth layer was cut open,
Three grains of corn were found.
Where to plant the corn?
On the hill where the chestnuts were growing.

剖开第六层鱼肚，
里面装着三粒黄豆子。
黄豆栽在什么地方？
长杨梅树的山上。

When the sixth layer was cut open,
Three grains of soybean were found.
Where to plant the soybean?
On the hill where the plum trees were growing.

剖开第七层鱼肚，
里面装着三粒南瓜子。
南瓜栽在什么地方？
长黄泡刺的地上。

When the seventh layer was cut open,
Three grains of pumpkin were found.
Where to plant the pumpkin?
On the ground where the yellow berry thorns were stretching.

剖开第八层鱼肚，
里面装着三粒麻子。
麻栽在什么地方？
淌水的冲沟旁。

When the eighth layer was cut open,
Three grains of hemp were found.
Where to plant the hemp?
Beside the gully where water was dripping.

昂煞息思
Angshaxisi

剖开第九层鱼肚，	When the ninth layer was cut open,
里面装着各种树种。	A variety of tree seeds were found.
树种撒在什么地方？	Where to cast the tree seeds?
撒在所有的山上。	All over the mountains.

剖开第十层鱼肚， When the tenth layer was cut open,
里面装着各种草种。 A variety of grass seeds were found.
草种撒在什么地方？ Where to cast the grass seeds?
地上水里草会长。 On the ground or in the water.

五谷籽种都有了， All grain seeds were now recovered,
各种树种都有了， All tree seeds were now recovered,
各种草种都有了， All grass seeds were now recovered,
一样种也不差了。 People were short of nothing now.

人们年年栽五谷， Every year people planted their corn;
年年把种收藏， Every year people stored their seeds.
一年一年传下去， Thus the seeds were passed on
一代一代不绝种。 From generation to generation.

人们把树种撒在所有的山上， People cast the tree seed over the hills,
人们把草种撒在地上水里， And grass seeds across water and land.
从此山山岭岭长了树， Soon the hills abounded in trees,
地上水里到处长了草。 And grass was thick in water and land.

大地穿上绿衣裳，
莫米见了心里老实喜欢。
树木世世代代不绝种，
杂草祖祖辈辈不绝种。
众：萨—萨！

The earth was dressed in green,
Which pleased Momi very much.
Trees and grass would thrive forever
From one generation to another.
Chorus: Sah-Sah!

阿资资斗
Azizidou*

---

* 阿资资斗：哈尼语，即砍树计日。
  Azizidou means counting days by cutting trees.

十二奴局 // Twelve Nujus

萨啦阿依——	Sala Ayi–
远远的烘阿宗娘①地方，	Far in the area of Hong'a①,
住着一家十兄妹，	There lived a family with ten siblings.
九个哥哥成了家，	Nine brothers all had married,
小妹的名字叫尖收。	And the youngest girl was named Jianshou.
尖收勤劳性平和，	Industrious and mild-tempered,
一天给九个哥哥背九次水，	Jianshou carried water and collected firewood
一天给九个哥哥砍九次柴，	For each brother, nine times every day.
每次背的水一样清，	Every bucket of water she carried was equally clear;
每次砍的柴一样多。	Every bundle of wood she collected was equally heavy.
九个哥哥是勾心，	The nine brothers were mean,
把小妹尖收当牛马：	Treating their sister Jianshou as a slave:
米饭不给她吃，	They provided no food for her to eat,
新衣不给她穿，	No new clothes for her to wear,
狗咬不帮她吆。	No help when she was under attack by dogs.
尖收一日哭三回天不黑，	Three times in one day she cried;
尖收一夜醒三次天不亮，	Three times in one night she woke up.

---

① 烘阿宗娘：烘阿，古地名；宗娘，旁边的意思。

① An ancient place.

阿资资斗
Azizidou

尖收再也熬不下去了,	Jianshou could no longer endure the misery,
只得拿起讨饭棍,	But picked up a beggar's stick,
淌着眼泪离开家。	And left her home in tears.
她从高山讨到江河汇集的海边,	She begged from the hill to the sea where rivers converged;
她从海边讨到江河源头的高山。	She begged from the sea to the hills where rivers began.

有天尖收讨饭来到阿姆山, One day Jianshou arrived at Mount Amu,
面前有块望不到边的大田, And found a boundless field,
大田水口七筹宽。 On which there was a gutter seven zithers wide.
尖收拄着讨饭棍过田埂。 Walking across the ridge with her stick,
跳过田水口, Jianshou tried to leap over the gutter,
拄棍生了根, But her supporting stick got rooted
忽然变成一棵大青树。 And turned into a huge banyan tree all of a sudden.

大青树遮住了天, The tree clouded the sky
大青树盖住了地。 And shaded the earth.
太阳看不见了, The sun became invisible,
月亮看不见了, And the moon was also gone.
白昼变成了黑夜。 Bright days turned into dark nights.
尖收倒在地, Jianshou fell to the ground,
化作"哒嘟哒"①。 Turning into Daduda①.

地下漆黑一片, The ground was all pitch black,

---

① 哒嘟哒:一种夜鸟。 ① A kind of nocturnal bird.

不知东边在哪方，	And people lost their sense of direction,
不知西边在哪方，	Unable to tell the east from the west.
人有眼睛像没有眼睛一样。	People were as if without eyes.
人们把火把绑在牛角上犁田，	In order to plough the field,
人们把火把拴在羊角上犁地。	People tied torches to the horns of cattle and goats.
可是栽下的庄稼不会长，	But neither would the crops grow,
栽下的秧苗不会结谷子。	Nor would the planted seedlings yield millet.
沉沉的黑夜无尽头，	The dark night seemed endless,
世上的人们难忍受，	So unbearable for people in the world.
男女老少跪在地，	Everybody on their knees
苦苦向天神哭诉：	Cried to the ruling god in bitterness:
"仁慈的莫米呀，	"Merciful Momi,
你为何把太阳月亮收起，	Why do you put away the sun and the moon?
我们活不下去了，	We can't live without them,
快把太阳月亮放出来。"	Please do let them out."
男人的喉咙哭哑了，	Men's throats became hoarse crying,
女人的眼泪哭干了，	And women had dried all their tears.
可是莫米没有回音，	But nothing came back from Momi,
太阳月亮还是出不来。	While the sun and the moon were still missing.
太阳到哪里去了？	Where did the sun go?
月亮到哪里去了？	Where did the moon go?

阿资资斗
Azizidou

世上的人们一起商量，	People all over the world decided
决定派百兽到树顶瞧瞧，	To send animals to check on the tree top,
找回太阳和月亮，	To find the sun and the moon,
寻回生存的光明。	And bring back the light of life.

第一次派出灵巧的猴子，　　First the nimble monkey was sent out,
猴子磨破肉皮爬上树顶。　　Wearing out its skin to climb to the top of the tree.
原来天还是晴朗，　　　　　Apparently it was still a sunny day,
日月星辰仍旧放光。　　　　All stars still shining in their right places.
贪玩的猴子呀，　　　　　　But the playful monkey,
忘记主人的嘱咐，　　　　　Forgetting what his master had told him,
三年不转路，　　　　　　　Failed to return in three years,
一去不回音。　　　　　　　As if it had vanished into thin air.

人们又派出机灵的松鼠，　　Then the smart squirrel was sent out,
松鼠使尽力气爬上树顶。　　Who spared no effort to climb up to the top.
原来天还是晴朗，　　　　　Apparently it was still a sunny day,
日月星辰仍旧放光。　　　　All stars still shining in their right places.
松鼠被太阳迷住，　　　　　The squirrel was fascinated by the sun,
高兴得在树枝上跳舞。　　　Dancing on the branches with joy.
贪玩的松鼠呀，　　　　　　The naughty squirrel,
忘记主人的嘱咐，　　　　　Forgetting what his master had told him,
三年不转路，　　　　　　　Failed to return in three years,
一去不回音。　　　　　　　As if it had vanished into thin air.

十二奴局 // Twelve Nujus

人们又派出劲飞的野鸡，	Then the flying pheasant was sent out,
野鸡七天飞到树顶。	Who took seven days to fly to the tree top.
原来天还是晴朗，	Apparently it was still a sunny day,
日月星辰仍然放光。	All stars still shining in their right places.
野鸡被美景迷住了，	The pheasant was fascinated by the scene,
放开嗓子在树上啼鸣。	Chirping on the tree to her heart's content.
贪玩的野鸡呀，	The playful pheasant,
忘记主人的嘱咐，	Forgetting what her master had told her,
三年不转路，	Failed to return in three years,
一去不回音。	As if it had vanished into thin air.

人们又派出飞得最快的蝙蝠，	People then sent out the swiftest bat,
蝙蝠像箭一样飞到树顶。	Who flew like an arrow to the tree top.
原来天还是晴朗，	Apparently it was still a sunny day,
日月星辰仍然放光。	All stars still shining in their right places.
蝙蝠被太阳刺瞎了眼睛，	The bat was blinded by the sunlight,
爬在树枝上不动。	Curling on the branches motionless.
三年不转路，	He failed to return in three years,
一去不回音。	As if it had vanished into thin air.

日子一年一年过去了，	Time passed year after year,
人们望穿了双眼。	And people had strained their eyes waiting.
请来燕子又去打听，	They asked the swallow to inquire,

阿资资斗
Azizidou

并向它许下了重愿：	While making a big promise:
"燕子呀！	"Dear swallow!
你快去快飞回，	You'd better go fast and return promptly,
想尽办法查明原因，	And find out the reason whatever it takes.
来日人间得到光明，	The day when the world sees light again,
给你同人住一间房！"	You will have a room to be shared with human!"
三日不到燕子飞回，	The swallow flew back within three days,
把喜讯告诉人们：	Informing the people of the good news:
"树上边天气晴朗，	"It's bright and sunny above the tree,
日月星辰放光明。"	All stars shining in their right places."
人们问燕子，	People asked the swallow,
为哪样光照不到地上？	Why couldn't the light be shed on the ground?
燕子只顾欢喜，	The swallow was too excited
忘记查原因，	To look for the reason.
"吱吱"地说了半天，	She tweeted and tweeted,
一样原因也说不明。	But could not provide anything solid.
人们又请蜜蜂去查看，	People then asked the bee to inquire,
并向它许下了重愿：	While making a big promise:
"金蜂呀！	"Golden bee!
你快去快飞回，	You'd better go fast and return promptly,
想尽办法查明原因，	And find out the reason whatever it takes.

十二奴局 // Twelve Nujus

来日人间得到光明，	The day when the world sees light again,
给你筑巢挂屋檐！"	Your nest will be allowed to hang below our roof!"
三日不到蜂飞回，	The bee flew back within three days,
向人们献了一个巧计：	Offering a smart plan:
"是树叶挡住了日月，	"Blocking the sun and the moon are the leaves.
射穿树叶见光辉！"	Shoot them, and the world will see the light again!"
各族兄弟围拢来，	Men of all ethnic groups came around,
推举仆拉①猎手阿戛：	Spurring on Aga the famous Pula[①] hunter.
"勇敢的阿戛，	"Brave Aga,
你是世间最神的射手，	You are the sharpest shooter in the world.
快握起奶桑木做的弯弓，	Grab your bow made from mulberry wood,
快扎上细牢的麻线，	Fasten it with fine strong thread,
快配上最好的弩箭，	Put on your best arrows,
施展出你高强的本领。"	Now it's time to show your talent."
千只眼不眨，	Hundreds of unblinking eyes stared
齐望阿戛的弩箭；	At Aga's arrows;
万颗心屏住，	Thousands of hearts skipped a beat,
贴向阿戛的弓弦。	As if they were on Aga's bowstring.
阿戛拉满弓弦，	Aga pulled the bow,
弩箭飞出似闪电。	And the arrow flew out like lightning.
一声轰隆震响，	With a thunderous noise,

---

① 仆拉：彝族支系，自称。　　① A branch of the Yi people.

阿资资斗
Azizidou

一张牛皮大的树叶落下地。	A big cowskin-sized leaf fell down.
人们见到一线阳光,	People saw a ray of sunshine,
欢呼声震响山冈。	And loud cheers went up all over the hill.

九十九寨的哈尼,	Hani people from ninety-nine villages,
九十九寨的彝家,	Yi people from ninety-nine villages,
九十九寨的汉人,	Han people from ninety-nine villages,
九十九寨的傣家……	Dai people from ninety-nine villages,
大家聚拢来商量,	All gathered to form a plan
要砍倒大树见日月。	To remove the tree and bring back the stars.

九千人拿刀砍,	Nine thousand people cut with knives,
九千人用斧劈,	Nine thousand slashed with axes.
九千人拉大锯,	Nine thousand pulled big saws,
九千人用凿子凿,	Nine thousand chopped with chisels.
各族兄弟齐心合力,	All their efforts were combined
像林中的老藤扭在一起。	Like vines interwoven in the woods.
汗珠滚落汇成小河,	Beads of sweat converged into a river,
砍树的叮当声传百里。	And the jingle of chopping rang hundreds of miles away.

日头落下山,	At the time of sunset,
大树砍出一道口。	A gash was formed on the trunk.
心想只要砍几日,	All thought it would take only a few days
大树就会倒在地,	Before the tree fell down.

可是二日一早起来看，	But when they checked it the next morning,
树上的斧口又长齐了。	The wound in the tree had healed perfectly.
再日砍，三日砍，	They kept chopping in the following days,
砍了七天都一样：	But it was all the same seven days in a row:
白天大树见裂口，	Daytime labor left the tree with a wound,
二天起来一看无缝隙。	Which would disappear overnight.
遮天大树没有砍倒，	The towering tree remained intact,
背来的粮食吃完了。	But people were now out of food.
人们都回去背粮食，	They went back home to get food,
留下一个傣家守工具。	Leaving behind a Dai man on watch.
这个傣家人，	This Dai man on watch
睡在树旁一个石洞里，	Slept in a cave beside the tree.
到了夜半三更时，	In the middle of the night,
一阵说话声把他从梦中吵醒，	He was woken by voices.
他竖起耳朵仔细听，	He was all ears to learn from
原来是守林的鬼神在议论：	The whispers of the forest spirits:
不要怕，不要怕，	"Don't panic, don't panic,
不抹鸡屎砍不倒大树。	The tree will never be cut down without chicken droppings."
大伙背着粮食转来了，	When people came back with food,
傣家把听到的奥秘告诉大家。	The Dai man shared the secret.
大伙听了心里非常高兴，	Everyone was very happy to know,
派人回家背来鸡屎。	

阿资资斗
Azizidou

        And hurriedly had the droppings ready.

人们在刀口上抹上鸡屎，	Applying the droppings to the edges of their axes,
砍树像切萝卜一样，	Now people chopped the tree as if it were carrots.
一刀更比一刀深。	As the cut advanced deeper and deeper,
千万刀砍下树摇晃，	The tree became unstable after thousands of strikes.
大树随着一阵嘎嘎声，	Then with creaks and booms,
天崩地裂倒下地。	It fell down shattering the earth.
遮天大树砍倒了，	Now the towering tree had collapsed,
阳光照到大地上。	And the sun was back shining.
百鸟飞出来唱歌，	Birds were flying and singing,
百兽跑出来跳跃，	And beasts were running and leaping.
人们哟！	All the people were happily celebrating
像过年过节一样欢乐。	Like during the new year festival.
遮天大树砍倒了，	Now that the towering tree had collapsed,
人们细细数了数：	The people took time to count:
百丈高的大树，	The tree, thousand feet tall,
共有十二杈，	Had a total of twelve boughs,
后来人们把一年定为十二个月；	So be twelve the number of months in a year;
每一杈上长三十根树枝，	Each bough had thirty twigs,
后来人们把一个月定为三十天；	So be thirty the number of days in a month;
每根树枝上长三百六十片叶子，	Three hundred and sixty leaves grew on each branch,

后来人们把一年定为三百六十天。 So be it the number of days in a year.

遮天大树砍倒了， Now the towering tree had collapsed,
却把大地打碎了。 Smashing the earth into pieces.
过去的大地， The land of the past,
是平平的一整块， Used to be a whole flat piece,
跟阿姆山一样高， High as Mount Amu,
跟阿姆山山顶一样平。 Flat as its hilltop.
大树倒下时， When the tree collapsed,
把大地打成数不尽的坑坑洼洼， Countless potholes took shape,
这些坑坑洼洼哟， Which later turned into
后来变成了数不尽的江河湖海。 Numerous rivers and lakes.
众：萨—萨！ Chorus: Sah-Sah!

阿扎多拉
Azhaduola*

---

* 阿扎多拉：即火的起源。
　Azhaduola means the origin of fire.

十二奴局 // Twelve Nujus

萨啦阿依——	Sala Ayi–
天上没有太阳，	Were it not for the sun in the sky,
世间分不出白天黑夜来；	There would've been no days or nights.
地上没有水，	Were it not for the water on the ground,
田地里的庄稼不会栽；	Crops would've not grown in the fields.
世上没有火，	Were it not for the fire in the world,
人类就不会发展到这一代。	Humans would not have evolved to this age.
红彤彤的火，	Red fire is indispensable
世间的人一个也离不开。	For every single person in this world.
很古很古的时候，	In the ancient past,
我们的先祖连房子都不会盖，	Our ancestors knew nothing of house-building.
到处乱睡觉，	They slept in the wilderness,
人成了老虎豹子的饭菜。	At risk of being preyed on by tigers and leopards.
那时候虎豹比人多，	Outnumbered by the beasts,
宽宽的地上人不敢在，	People did not dare to stay on the broad land.
冷天住在石洞里，	They lived in stone caves on cold days,
热天搬到树上在。	And moved up to the trees in hot weather.
冷天住在石洞暖和和，	It was cozy dwelling in the caves on cold days,
热天住在树上好凉快。	And pretty cool living in trees in hot weather.
不怕热和冷，	For all the comforts provided by their shelters,

阿扎多拉
Azhaduola

不怕老虎豹子抬，	And all the safety away from tigers and leopards,
只是蟒蛇凶，	They were still under threat from pythons,
人天天要受到伤害。	Who were evil and harmful;
我们的先祖，	Our ancestors found it unbearable
住在石洞和树上日子难挨。	To live in caves and in trees.

我们的先祖，　　　　　　Back then our ancestors
那时候不会栽棉花，　　　Knew nothing of cotton-growing,
没有棉和线，　　　　　　Much less of spinning cotton into thread;
葛麻也不会采，　　　　　They knew nothing of making linen from kudzu.
白天没有裤子穿，　　　　So they had no pants to wear in the daytime,
晚上睡觉没有被子盖。　　And no blankets when sleeping at night.

撕来芭蕉叶作衣裤穿，　　Banana leaves were used as clothes,
掳来茅草作被子盖。　　　While thatch was heaped up to make blankets,
热天在茅草堆上睡，　　　On top of which they slept when it was hot,
冷天在茅草堆里埋。　　　In between which they rested on cold days.
只是芭蕉叶不牢，　　　　But the banana leaves were not firm enough,
身上很快被树枝戳坏。　　Easily pierced by sticking boughs;
我们的先祖，　　　　　　Our ancestors suffered a lot
穿芭蕉叶的日子艰难。　　During the days of wearing banana leaves.

我们的先祖，　　　　　　Back then our ancestors
那时候谷子还不会栽，　　Knew nothing about millet planting,

十二奴局 // Twelve Nujus

不会养猪鸡，	Or pig and chicken raising.
生活也不会安排。	They had no idea what to do with their lives.
没有吃的，	When they needed food,
大家上山把马鹿麂子逮，	All went up the hill to hunt muntjac deer;
马鹿麂子撵不着，	And if not successful,
就到山上采野果野菜。	They picked wild fruits and vegetables instead.

马鹿麂子味道虽然好，	Though muntjac deer tasted good,
有时候却几日逮不来。	They were not available every day.
遍山的野菜野果，	Though wild fruits were all over the hill,
有时候也会全部枯败。	There were days when they were all withered.
到了那时候，	Those days of scarcity
人们就遭了大灾，	Were miserably disastrous.
命小的就到阴间，	Unlucky ones died,
命大的就在世上留下来。	While lucky ones survived.

我们的先祖，	Back then our ancestors
那时候还没有造出火来，	Knew nothing of fire.
天冷的时候，	When it was cold,
像猪一样乱草堆里埋。	People were snug in the hay like pigs.
逮来了麂鹿，	When a muntjac deer was caught,
像豹子一样撕着吃生肉。	They tore and ate the meat raw like leopards.
野菜采来了，	When the wild plants were gathered,
像牛马一样直往嘴里塞。	They stuffed their mouths like cattle and horses.

阿扎多拉
Azhaduola

在那古老的年代，	In that ancient time,
整个大地一片青翠，	The whole land was verdant.
蕨蕨草像大青树一样高，	Ferns were as high as trees,
杆杆粗的有好几围。	With stems several arm lengths thick.
肥壮的马鹿麂子，	Fat muntjac deer
成群地在树荫底下睡，	Slept in the shade of trees in herds.
人们拿着石头和棍棒，	With stones and sticks,
一起去把马鹿麂子围。	People went to surround them.
人们打死的马鹿麂子多了，	As more and more deer were captured,
麂鹿吓得向遥远的地方隐退。	The living ones fled to the remote areas frightened.
没有马鹿和麂子，	Once they were all gone,
我们的先祖就只好又搬家，	Our ancestors had to move too,
搬到有马鹿麂子的森林里。	To the forest where those beasts dwelt.
马鹿麂子又跑了，	Again the deer ran away,
人们又把家搬一回。	And again people moved afterwards.
马鹿麂子，	The poor muntjac deer
整天被人撵得不停腿，	Were chased around the clock
顾不上吃一口青草，	Without even a break for eating grass,
顾不得喝一口清水。	Or a moment of drinking water.
日子过得不安宁，	In this discomfort of life,
天天向莫米控诉人的罪。	They resorted to Momi for justice.

十二奴局 // Twelve Nujus

莫米被吵得发了怒，	Irritated by the complaints,
立即丢下了几颗巨大的火雷。	Momi immediately dropped a couple of huge lightning bolts.
无边的森林着了火，	When the boundless forest caught fire,
火焰成了吃人的魔鬼。	The flame became a human-devouring devil,
老幼烧成了火炭，	Burning people of all ages into charcoal,
枯木朽木烧成了白灰。	And deadwood into ashes.
人们吓得胆战心惊，	People were so scared,
急忙向遥远的地方逃避。	Fleeing to the distance in haste.
为了活命，	In order to survive,
大家去把马鹿麂子追。	They ran after the muntjac deer.
马鹿麂子逃向遥远的地方，	As the deer were heading into the distance,
人们尾着紧紧在后边追。	People just followed closely behind.
马鹿麂子不停步，	As the deer were running nonstop,
人们也紧追不歇脚。	People were after them likewise.
追到雷火烧过的林地，	On reaching the forest earlier burned in fire,
烧死的麂鹿被乌鸦包围。	They found burned deer surrounded by crows.
人们驱走了乌鸦，	People drove away the crows,
撕碎了烧熟的麂鹿脚，	Ripped off the burned deer legs,
放到嘴里边一嚼，	Put them into their mouths,
觉得比吃生肉更有味，	And found that compared to raw meat,
比生肉好吃，比生肉香脆。	They were more tasty and crispy.

阿扎多拉
Azhaduola

我们的先祖，	One of our ancestors,
有个叫司米锐，	Whose name was Simirui,
吃了火烧肉，	After eating the burned meat
感到肉味老实美，	That was really delicious,
知道火有很大用处，	Realized that the fire would be of great use,
就约大家一起去把火尾。	And suggested for everyone to grab the fire.
找遍雷火烧过的地方，	They scoured every place that had been burned,
寻遍了东南西北，	South and north, east and west,
一点火也没有了，	But there was no single spark left,
只剩下一堆堆的草木灰。	Except for piles of ashes.

找火找不着，	Unable to find the fire,
就求莫米把火恩赐给人类。	They turned to Momi for his mercy.
男女老少，	Men and women, old and young,
不知给莫米磕头磕了多少回，	Lost count kowtowing to Momi.
天上的莫米，	But Momi in the heaven
却一点火也不肯给。	Granted no response at all.

司米锐的后代，	One day this offspring of Simirui
有个叫锐腿雷的，	With the name of Ruituilei,
有天领着大家撵麂鹿，	Was leading in the chase for muntjac deer.
麂鹿跑进深深的林子内；	The deer ran deep into the dense woods,
林深草密虎豹多，	Where most ferocious beasts dwelt,

十二奴局 // Twelve Nujus

人们不敢再进林子里去追。	And the chasers dared not to go any further.
锐腿雷领着一伙人，	Ruituilei led his fellowmen up to the hill,
到山上滚石头把麂鹿催。	Planning to flush out the deer with rolling stones.

我们的先祖锐腿雷，	Our ancestor Ruituilei
抱来的一大块石头亮又白，	Picked a big rock bright and white,
用力往山下一滚，	And pushed it hard down the hill,
山坡上冒起了一大堆尘灰。	Blowing up a cloud of dust along the slope.
白石头狠狠砸在一棵树干上，	As the white rock smashed into a trunk,
震得大地抖了抖；	The ground shook and trembled
干树冒起了青烟，	Smoke arose from the trunk,
干树起火红焰飞。	Which soon was blazing with fire.

见到红彤彤的火，	Seeing the red flames,
大家立即往地上跑。	People all ran down the hill.
感谢天上的莫米，	They were so grateful to Momi,
把火赐给了人类。	For letting humans have fire finally.
大家笑呵呵，	Everybody happily
紧紧围住锐腿雷，	Gathered around Ruituilei,
夸他求来了莫米的火，	Who brought the fire from Momi,
称赞他有无穷的智慧。	And praised him for his originality.

马鹿麂子顾不着了，	Muntjac deer put aside,
大家跑去看火堆。	People all went to see the fire;

阿扎多拉
Azhaduola

大火烧得旺，	The fire was burning,
大家都感到非常欣慰。	And everyone felt gratified.
大家齐动手，	All contributed their effort,
搬来干柴直往火里堆。	Piling wood up in the fire.
野火烧过了，	So when the wildfire died down,
地上留下了火一大堆。	People still had fire on the ground.
天天往火里堆干柴，	People kept piling up wood,
大大的火堆日日火焰飞。	And the fires were burning all day long.
人们白天上山撵麂鹿，	They went up hill hunting in the day,
晚上在火堆里烧麂鹿腿。	And grilled deer legs at night.
烧熟的麂鹿肉，	The burnt deer meat
大家吃着非常有味，	Was very delicious;
吃到肚子里，	The fragrant smell
香透了心和肺。	Gratified their hearts.
天天往火里添干柴，	People kept piling up wood,
大大的火堆日日火焰飞。	And the fires were burning all day long.
凶恶的蟒蛇不敢来，	Vicious pythons dared not to come close,
残暴的虎豹也不敢来追。	And brutal tigers and leopards were kept away.
黑漆漆的夜晚，	In the dark night,
人就躺在火堆周围，	People lay around the fire,
个个睡得热和和，	All having a warm sleep,
人人睡得甜又美。	Sweet and comfortable.

十二奴局 // Twelve Nujus

人们有了火，	With fire in their hands,
温暖的日子甜醉了心房。	People's lives became warm and sweet.
吃得好来睡得香，	Good food and sound sleep
男人女人身体健壮。	Made healthy men and women.
女人生下小孩一大窝，	Women became fertile,
男人们个个喜洋洋。	And men happy and satisfied.
小孩一天天长大，	Children grew up day by day,
地上的人越来越兴旺。	And the human race was thriving.
生活在地上的人们，	People who lived on the earth
忘记了莫米的好心肠，	Forgot all of Momi's kindness.
撵得麂鹿不祭献，	They failed to offer sacrifices after hunting,
男女不分白天黑夜睡在一起。	And slept around whenever they wanted.
天上的莫米发了怒，	Momi's anger was kindled,
把大水降到了地上。	So he poured down water to the ground.
红彤彤的火被浇熄了，	The red flames were put out,
人们个个哭得泪汪汪。	Leaving people all in tears.
没有红彤彤的火，	Without the fire,
地上的人们遭了祸殃。	People on the ground suffered;
麂鹿肉虽肥，	Fat as the deer meat was,
生撕硬嚼味道不甜香。	It tasted rough and unpalatable.
男女老少哟，	People of all ages

阿扎多拉
Azhaduola

又成了老虎豹子的菜饭。 Once again became prey of the beasts.
过着苦难的日子, They led a miserable life,
心田积满冰和霜。 With hearts full of ice and frost.

男女老少齐跪下, People of all ages on their knees
把麂子马鹿肉献上, Offered muntjac deer meat as sacrifices.
向莫米认罪过, They confessed their guilt to Momi,
求莫米把红彤彤的火赐尝。 And begged him to give back the fire.

慈祥的莫米, Merciful Momi
开口对人们讲: Kindly told the people:
红彤彤的火种, The red precious fire
早已放到了地上; Was already put on the earth;
只要大家守规矩, As long as they behaved,
天天把莫米记心房, And kept Momi in their minds,
下功夫去寻找, They would find it sparkling
火种会闪出亮光。 If they searched hard enough.

人们牢记莫米的话, Bearing these words in mind,
到处去寻找火光。 People set out to look for the spark.
寻遍了东西南北, North and south, east and west,
找遍了四面八方, All directions were searched.
火种不得见, Unable to find the fire,
人们都感到非常悲伤。 People felt very sad.

十二奴局 // Twelve Nujus

人们找不到火种，	Unable to find the fire,
像块石头压住了心房。	People were all heavy-hearted.
锐腿雷领着大家，	Ruituilei led them again,
来到当年滚石头的山上，	Back to the stone-rolling hill.
寻来块块大白石，	They kept pushing white rocks
不停地直朝山脚滚放。	Down toward the hill bottom,
山脚不见起火烟，	But smoke was never seen rising,
山脚不见起火光。	And the fire never started.

可怜的人们，	These poor people,
心里装着无限的希望，	With infinite hope in their minds,
又找来一块块大白石，	Kept pushing large white rocks,
一次次直朝山脚滚放。	Down toward the bottom time and again.
砸倒森林一大片，	A large area of the forest was smashed,
砸得尘土满天飞扬，	And clouds of dust blew up in the air,
一丝火烟也没起，	But no single wisp of smoke was seen rising,
一线火光也不见亮。	And no single spark started.

找不到火种心不死，	People wouldn't give up
人们又连续把石头滚放。	But kept rolling stones.
滚了一天又一天，	Day after day,
滚了一趟又一趟。	Time and again.
可怜的人们，	These poor people

阿扎多拉
Azhaduola

眼睛直盯着山脚看，	Kept staring at the hill bottom,
仍然不见一丝火烟，	But no single wisp of smoke was seen rising,
仍然不见一线火光。	No single spark started.
白天滚了心不死，	Despite the failure in the day,
接着晚上又去把白石头滚放。	People kept rolling stones at night.
白石头顺着山坡一滚下，	As the white stone rolled down the slope,
山脚立即闪现出一道火光。	A light of fire flashed down the hill.
人们高兴了，	People were wild with joy,
立即跑到山脚去观看，	Running fast, down to see.
看不到红红的火焰，	There was no sign of fire at all,
人们感到非常失望。	And people were disappointed.
突然看见草丛里，	All of sudden in the grass,
闪着一点微微的火光，	A dim light was spotted glittering.
锐腿雷轻轻一抓，	Ruituilei grabbed it gently to find
原来火在一蓬绒草上。	The spark on a patch of fluffy grass.
莫米恩赐的火种，	The fire granted by Momi
原来放在这个地方。	Turned out to be placed here.
可怜的人们，	These poor people
心中升起了无限的希望。	Were now filled with infinite hope.
大家扯来毛茸茸的草，	They gathered more fluffy grass,
把珍贵的火种引上。	To be kindled by the precious spark.
一团团的绒草，	Piles of grass

火烧得越来越旺。	Fueled the fire;
突然腾起了火焰，	Then the flame leaped up,
闪出了亮亮的火光。	Flickering bright light.
大家又搬来一堆堆干柴，	People then gathered piles of dry wood,
把火引到大大的干柴堆上。	Which were kindled to build a big fire.
大火燃起来了，	Now they had the fire,
火光照亮了四面八方。	Shedding light in all directions.
蟒蛇吓得躲起来了，	Pythons were scared and hid themselves,
虎豹不敢再到人身边。	While tigers and leopards dared not come close.
男女老少，	Men and women, old and young,
睡着心里暖洋洋；	Slept feeling warm.
火烧麂鹿肉，	They ate grilled deer meat,
吃着嘴里肚里处处香。	Tasty smells running from mouth to belly.
红彤彤的火，	The red fire
是人类生存的希望。	Is the hope for human survival.
不能再让火浇灭，	Never let the fire out,
不然人又要遭受祸殃。	Or people would suffer again.
把火搬回石洞里，	Move the fire into the cave,
添上干柴把火烧旺，	And fuel it with dry wood.
用烧出来的火灰，	In the ashes from the burning,
把火种好好埋藏。	The spark will be kept carefully.
人在搬家时，	When you move,
首先不忘把火种带上；	Never forget to bring the spark along;

阿扎多拉
Azhaduola

到了新住处，	At the new home,
要先把火引着烧旺。	The first thing is to start up the fire.
从今以后哟，	From that day on,
祖先就靠小小的火塘，	Through fireplaces of generations,
一代又一代，	Our ancestors passed the fire
把火传到了我们手上。	Down to our hands.
众：萨—萨！	Chorus: Sah-Sah!

阿匹松阿
Apisong'a*

---

* 阿匹松阿：哈尼族传说中的能人，即头人、工匠和贝玛。
  Apisong'a means three capable men.

十二奴局 // Twelve Nujus

萨啦阿依——
遥远的天边，
有三块宽宽的平地：
开头一块是白的，
中间一块是花的，
下面一块是红的。

那时有三棵大树，
分别长在三块平地上：
开头一棵是白的，
中间一棵是花的，
下面一棵是红的。

三棵大树上，
开着三朵老实好看的花：
开头一朵是白的，
中间一朵是花的，
下面一朵是红的。

三朵花上有三个窝，
三个窝里有三个蛋：
开头一个是白的，

Sala Ayi–
In the distant horizon,
There were three wide plains:
The first of which was white,
The middle mixed-colored,
And the last one red.

There were three gigantic trees,
Growing on each of the three plains:
The first of which was white,
The middle mixed-colored,
And the last one red.

On the three trees,
Three beautiful flowers were blooming:
The first of which was white,
The middle mixed-colored,
And the last one red.

Three nests were found in the flowers,
Each with an egg in it:
The first of which was white,

阿匹松阿
Apisong'a

中间一个是花的，	The middle mixed-colored,
下面一个是红的。	And the last one red.

三个窝里三个蛋， Three eggs in three nests
三个蛋哟三种色， Were in different colors.
越看越神奇， They were a mystery for people
不知道是什么蛋。 Who had no idea about their names.
请问寨中放牛的小孩： They asked the cattle boy in the village:
"在遥远的天边， "In the distant horizon,
有三个不同色的蛋， There are three eggs different in color,
一个是白的， One white,
一个是花的， One mixed-colored,
一个是红的， One red.
知不知哪个是哪样蛋？ Do you know what eggs they are?
知不知会认蛋的人在哪里？" Or anybody who can tell?"

放牛的小孩看看天边， The cattle boy looked at the sky,
惊奇地睁大了眼睛， Widening his eyes in surprise;
像水牛甩尾一样把头摇， He shook his head the way a buffalo wags his tail,
连声说不知道。 Confessing that he didn't know.

请问放鸭的小孩： They went to the kid walking ducks:
"在遥远的天边， "In the distant horizon,
有三个不同色的蛋， There are three eggs different in color,

一个是白的，	One white,
一个是花的，	One mixed-colored,
一个是红的，	One red.
知不知哪个是哪样蛋？	Do you know what eggs they are?
知不知会认蛋的人在哪里？"	Or anybody who can tell?"
放鸭小孩看了看天边，	The duck-walking kid looked at the sky,
惊得张大了嘴巴，	His mouth gaping in surprise.
像风吹树梢一样把头摇，	He shook his head like wind through the trees,
连声说认不得。	Confessing that he didn't know.
请问寨中的老人：	They asked the elders in the village:
"在遥远的天边，	"In the distant horizon,
有三个不同色的蛋，	There are three eggs different in color,
一个是白的，	One white,
一个是花的，	One mixed-colored,
一个是红的。	One red.
知不知哪个是哪样蛋？	Do you know what eggs they are?
知不知会认蛋的人在哪里？"	Or anybody who can tell?"
寨中的老人一听，	The elders in the village
高高兴兴地告诉说：	Informed them happily:
"那是三个神蛋，	"Those are three divine eggs,
装着三种能人。	With three kinds of capable men inside.

阿匹松阿
Apisong'a

只要拿回蛋来抱，	Get back those eggs and hatch them,
白蛋会抱出头人来，	You will get a headman from the white egg,
花蛋会抱出贝玛来，	A beima from the mixed-colored one,
红蛋会抱出工匠来。"	And an artisan from the red one."
拿回三个神蛋，	The three divine eggs were brought back,
请大公鸡来抱，	And a rooster was asked to hatch them.
抱了一百天，	One hundred days passed by,
神蛋冷阴阴，	But the divine eggs remained cold,
抱死抱活不裂壳，	And the shells were yet to crack.
公鸡再也不敢抱了。	The rooster dared not go on.

请老母鸡来抱神蛋，　　Then a hen was asked to sit on the eggs.
母鸡抱了一百天，　　　One hundred days had passed by,
神蛋没有一点热气，　　But the divine eggs remained cold,
左抱右抱不裂壳，　　　While the shells were yet to crack.
母鸡吓得不敢再抱了。　So the hen dared not go on.

男人抱过了，　　Man tried to hatch them;
女人抱过了，　　Woman tried to hatch them;
狗也抱过了，　　Dog tried;
猫也抱过了，　　Cat tried,
鹅也抱过了，　　Goose tried,
鸭也抱过了，　　Duck tried,
神蛋还是冷阴阴，But the divine eggs remained cold,

神蛋还是不裂壳。	And the shells were yet to crack.
请教寨中的老人，	The elderly man in the village was consulted,
老人抬头指指天：	Who raised his head and pointed at the sky:
"三个神蛋天上来，	"As the divine eggs are from the heavens,
要请天上的太阳月亮抱。"	Only the sun and the moon can do the hatching."
太阳和月亮，	The sun and the moon
轮流抱神蛋。	Took turns to hatch the eggs:
白天太阳抱，	The sun took the dayshift,
晚上月亮抱，	And the moon the nightshift.
足足抱了九十天，	Ninety straight days later,
神蛋开始裂壳了。	The shells began to crack.
三个神蛋抱出来了：	From the three divine eggs,
白蛋抱出来了，	The white egg,
花蛋抱出来了，	The mixed-colored egg,
红蛋抱出来了。	And the red egg,
一个不同一个，	Each different from the other,
三个蛋抱出来三种能人。	Out hatched three capable men.
头人从白蛋里抱出来，	A headman came out of the white egg,
声音像打雷一样响；	Roaring like thunder;
贝玛从花蛋里抱出来，	A beima came out of the mixed-colored egg,

阿匹松阿
Apisong'a

有撮鸡毛挂在嘴角上；	With a bit of feather stuck to his mouth;
工匠从红蛋里抱出来，	An artisan came out of the red egg,
声音像拉风箱爆火花一样。	Who spoke like bellows blowing fire.

头人的名字叫龙波阿优①，　The headman was named Longboayou①,
长得高大又神采；　　　　　He was tall and handsome;
贝玛的名字叫龙斗阿沙②，　The beima was named Longdouasha②,
世上数他记性最好；　　　　He had the best memory in the world;
工匠的名字叫龙奴阿收③，　The artisan was named Longnuashou③,
两手粗壮心灵手巧。　　　　She was sturdy and smart.

头人住在哪里？　　　　Where did the headman live?
在仰者城④的金殿上。　In the Golden hall of the Yangzhe City④.
贝玛在哪里讲道理？　　Where did the beima spread his wisdom?
寨边长铁线草的路旁。　By the roadside where wiregrass grew.
工匠在哪里传手艺？　　Where did the artisan teach her craft?
寨门前有红土的地方。　On the red soil in front of the village gate.

头人分三等，　　Headmen were ranked in three classes,

---

① 龙波阿优：传说中第一个首领。
② 龙斗阿沙：传说中的第一个贝玛。
③ 龙奴阿收：传说中的第一个女师傅。
④ 仰者城：传说中的地名。

① The first headman.
② The first beima (priest).
③ The first female artisan.
④ A legendary place.

十二奴局 // Twelve Nujus

一等跟一等不一样：	Each different from the other.
一等头人头戴金帽子，	First-class headmen wore gold hats,
身穿长长的红衣裳，	As well as long red robes.
出出进进坐大轿，	They came and went in big sedan chairs,
仰者城里很威风。	Quite imposing in the city of Yangzhe.

二等头人头戴银帽子，　　Second-class headmen wore silver hats,
身穿长长的黑衣裳，　　　As well as long black robes.
出出进进骑大马，　　　　They came and went on horseback,
培包①镇上有随从。　　　Followed by attendants in the town of Peibao.

三等头人头戴铜帽子，　　Third-class headmen wore copper hats,
身穿长长的黑衣裳，　　　As well as long black robes.
走路拄一根手杖，　　　　They walked with sticks in hand,
窝龙龙坡、龙姿龙巴②查访。Inspecting their villages of Wolonglongpo and Longzilongba.

工匠分三等，　　　　　　Artisans were ranked in three classes,
一等跟一等不一样：　　　Each different from the other.
头等工匠手艺高，　　　　First-class artisans were highly skilled,
炼铜炼铁倒犁花，　　　　Capable of copper-smelting, iron-making and plowing.
手拿弯尺和墨斗，　　　　With scales and ink in hand,

---

① 培包：传说中的城镇名。
② 窝龙龙坡、龙姿龙巴：传说中的远古乡、村地名。

阿匹松阿
Apisong'a

盖新房时立柱子。	They erected pillars for new houses.
二等工匠有办法，	Second-class artisans were resourceful,
打制锄头斧子和镰刀，	Capable of forging hoes, axes and sickles.
手拿斧子和锯子，	With axes and saws in hand,
砍倒大树解成板。	They cut down trees and sawed them into planks.
三等工匠手灵巧，	Third-class artisans were dexterous.
砍倒竹子树，	They cut down bamboo trees
织出筛子、簸箕和背箩，	To weave sieves, dustpans and back baskets,
编制纸人和纸马。	And crafted paper people and horses.
自从世间有头人，	Thanks to the headman
天天给人断事情，	Who served justice,
吵闹打架的事少了，	Quarrels and fights were declining;
抢人杀人的事少了，	Robberies and murders were decreasing.
地方管得平平的，	Feeling safe in this well-managed place,
百姓好吃好在了。	People were able to enjoy their lives.
人们为了谢头人，	To express their thanks to the headman,
把最俏的女人送给他做老婆，	People sent him the prettiest woman as his wife,
把最贵重的东西送给他用，	The most expensive things for him to use,
把最好吃的东西拿给他享受。	And the most delicious food for him to taste.

自从世间有贝玛，	Thanks to the beima,
天天给人驱鬼治病。	Who evicted ghosts and healed people.
用黄泡刺挡住寨门，	Shielded the gate with yellow rubus thorns,
用灶灰堵住路口，	And armed the road with stove ash.
魔鬼害怕了，	The devils were terrified,
躲到深山悬崖去了。	And hid themselves in mountain cliffs.
寨子不闹鬼了，	The village was no longer haunted,
生病的人少了，	So fewer people got sick;
生出来的小娃长得大，	Babies could grow up to adulthood,
年纪大的老人活得长。	And the elders lived longer.

人们为了感谢贝玛，	To express their thanks to the beima,
把肉多的鸡腿牛腿送给他，	People sent him fat legs of chickens and cows,
把白米和银子送给他，	Rice and silver,
把新布送给他。	And newly woven fabrics.

自从世间有了工匠，	The artisan in this world
天天给人们做活计。	Did all kinds of work for people:
炼铜炼铁倒犁花，	Copper-smelting, iron-making and plowing;
打制锄头砍刀和斧子，	Forging hoes, axes and sickles;
编制背箩筛子和簸簸，	Weaving sieves, dustpans and back baskets,
砍来树木盖新房。	And cutting down trees to build houses.
有了铜铁做活省力气，	Copper and iron saved a lot of labor,
有了各种工具好栽田种地，	And the various tools helped a lot in farming.

阿匹松阿
Apisong'a

有了房子不怕风吹雨打，	Houses protected people from wind and rain,
百姓好吃好在过日子。	Who were able to enjoy their lives.

人们为了感谢工匠，
拿酒拿肉给他吃，
送谷送米养他的儿女，
拿出心来待工匠。

To express their thanks to the Artisan,
People presented him with meat and wine,
Corn and rice for him to raise his children,
Treating him with loyal hearts.

头人、贝玛和工匠，
一起生一起长的亲兄弟，
和和气气管人间，
百姓无灾无难安居乐业。

The headman, the beima and the artisan
Brothers born and raised together,
Ruled the world with kindness,
Freeing people from worry in work and life.

不知过了多少年，
不知过了多少代，
人们的心开始臭起来，
把头人、贝玛和工匠怨恨，
认为人间无灾难，
白白养活他们划不着。
村村寨寨吹起牛角号，
赶走了头人、贝玛和工匠。

Countless years later,
Countless generations later,
People's hearts began to stink,
Becoming resentful of the headman, the beima and
　　　the artisan.
As no disaster was seen in the world,
It seemed not worthwhile to support them for nothing;
Horns were blown in every village,
Demanding the departure of the headman, the beima
　　　and the artisan.

头人赶走了,	When the headman was gone,
人间出了大小事情没人断。	Disputes, big or small, were left unsettled.
不知过了多少天,	Countless days later,
不知过了多少年,	Countless years later,
人们互相吵架打起来,	People got into big conflicts,
人们互相争斗杀起来。	Fighting to kill each other.
没有头人来坐堂,	As there was no headman ruling,
一个管不着一个,	No one cared to compromise,
地方像冬天的大雾一样乱。	And the place became as chaotic as the winter fog.

贝玛赶走了,	As the beima was gone,
拦寨门的黄泡刺掉了。	The yellow rubus thorns at the gate withered.
不知过了多少天,	Countless days later,
不知过了多少年,	Countless years later,
成群魔鬼闯进寨子来吃人,	Devils broke into the village in groups;
疾病和灾难像秋天的树叶一样落下来。	Diseases and disasters fell like autumn leaves.

工匠赶走了,	As the artisan was gone,
寨门外的铁匠房倒了。	His workshop outside the village collapsed.
不知过了多少天,	Countless days later,
不知过了多少年,	Countless years later,
锄头斧子砍刀坏了没人修,	With hoes, axes and chopping tools in disrepair.
住的房子烂了没人盖,	And houses in bad shape,

阿匹松阿
Apisong'a

人们不会栽田种地了，	People were unable to farm,
人们不会安家过日子了。	Nor could they ever enjoy their lives.

世间的人哟，　　　　　　People in this world
没有头人不会在，　　　　Were ill at ease without the headman,
没有贝玛不会在，　　　　Ill at ease without the beima,
没有工匠不会在。　　　　Ill at ease without the artisan.
村村寨寨议论纷纷，　　　The word spread across villages,
男人女人来商量：　　　　As men and women were saying
要把头人请回来，　　　　That the headman should be invited back,
要把贝玛叫回来，　　　　The beima asked back,
要把工匠找回来。　　　　And the artisan found back.

去问寨中的老人，　　　　They asked the eldest man in the village,
头人、贝玛、工匠在哪里？　Where to find the headman, the beima, and the artisan?
老人摇摇头，　　　　　　The elder shook his head,
叹气不说话。　　　　　　Sighing instead of speaking.

去问河坝的傣家，　　　　They asked the Dai by the riverside,
头人、贝玛、工匠在哪里？　Where to find the headman, the beima, and the artisan?
傣家摇摇头，　　　　　　The Dai shook his head,
说他没见着。　　　　　　Saying that he had no idea.

十二奴局 // Twelve Nujus

去问做生意的汉人，	They asked the Han businessman,
头人、贝玛、工匠在哪里？	Where to find the headman, the beima, and the artisan?
汉人摇摇头，	The Han shook his head,
说他没有遇着。	Saying that he had not met any of them.

去问半山腰的彝家，　　They asked the Yi at the hillside,
头人、贝玛、工匠在哪里？　Where to find the headman, the beima, and the artisan?
彝家摇摇头，　　　　　The Yi shook his head,
说他没听说。　　　　　Saying that he never heard anything about them.

山鸡问过了，　　　　　The prairie chicken had been asked,
白鹇问过了，　　　　　And so had the silver pheasant.
画眉问过了，　　　　　The thrush had been asked,
斑鸠问过了，　　　　　And so had the dove.
个个都说没见着，　　　None of them had ever seen the three,
个个都说不知道。　　　Nor did they have any clue.

猴子问过了，　　　　　The monkey had been asked,
松鼠问过了，　　　　　And so had the squirrel;
野猪问过了，　　　　　The wild boar had been asked,
马鹿问过了，　　　　　And so had the red deer.
个个都说没遇着，　　　None of them had ever met the three,
个个都说不知道。　　　Nor did they have any clue.

阿匹松阿
Apisong'a

人们包着冷饭到处找,	People searched with cold rice balls,
人们大声喊着到处叫。	Shouting from place to place.
找遍了宽宽的河坝,	All the wide riversides had been searched,
听不到头人、贝玛、工匠的声音;	With no voice of the three ever heard.
找遍了所有的半山腰,	All the hillsides had been explored,
看不到头人、贝玛、工匠的脚迹;	With no footprint of them ever seen.
找遍了所有的高山,	All the mountains had been probed,
见不到头人、贝玛、工匠的影子。	With no trace of them ever found.

人们的心像水浇着一样冷了, People's hearts turned cold as if dampened,
人们的心像刺戳着一样难受了。 And painful as if on thorns.
男人的脖子哭哑了, Men got hoarse voices crying,
女人的眼泪哭干了。 And women dried up their tears.
恰恰这时候, Just at that time,
有只燕子从远处飞来。 There came a swallow flying from afar.
人们问燕子: People asked the swallow,
头人、贝玛、工匠在哪里? Where to find the headman, the beima and the artisan?

燕子站在树枝上, The swallow stood on one branch,
歪着头对人们说: Tilted his head and said:
"我飞遍了大地, "I've been flying through the earth
我飞过了大海, And across the sea.
头人、贝玛和工匠, The headman, the beima and the artisan
只听说过没见着。" Are things I've heard of but never seen."

十二奴局 // Twelve Nujus

人们没有办法了，	At their wits' end,
苦苦请求燕子说：	People begged the swallow:
"没有头人、贝玛和工匠，	"Without the headman, the beima and the artisan,
我们一天也不会过日子，	We don't know what to do with our lives.
求你可怜我们，	Have mercy on us please,
帮我们请回头人、贝玛、工匠来。"	And help bring them back."

燕子同情人们，　　　　　　　In sympathy the swallow flew away
便飞去找头人、贝玛和工匠。　To find the headman, the beima and the artisan.
整整过了一年，　　　　　　　After a full year,
燕子飞回来告诉人们：　　　　It came back to tell the people:
"头人、贝玛和工匠找着了，　"I've found the headman, the beima and the artisan
住在遥远的天边边，　　　　　On the distant horizon.
三弟兄栽田种地有吃有穿，　　The three brothers labor to support themselves,
不愿回来给你们讨人嫌。"　　Unwilling to come back only to be hated."

人们听了又悲又喜，　　　　　Filled with sweet sorrow,
要求燕子发善心：　　　　　　People begged the swallow for mercy:
"你给我们带带路，　　　　　"Would you please lead us the way,
我们亲自去请他们。"　　　　So we will invite them back ourselves?"

燕子心软了，　　　　　　　　The swallow softened
展开翅膀飞在前面带路。　　　And spread its wings to lead the way.

阿匹松阿
Apisong'a

人们跟在后面，	People followed behind,
跨过了数不尽的江河，	Across countless rivers,
翻过了数不清的高山，	Over countless mountains.
足足走了一年，	A full year later,
来到三弟兄住的天边。	They arrived where the three lived.

人们见到三个能人，　　　　Upon seeing the three capable men,
亲切地恳求他们说：　　　　People begged them sincerely:
"尊敬的头人、贝玛和工匠，　"Honored headman, beima and artisan,
过去是我们错了，　　　　　We used to be so wrong,
被泥巴糊住眼好坏不分，　　As if blinded by the mud.
没有你们我们不会过日子，　Without you we don't know what to do,
请你们回到我们那里去。"　Please come back to our place."

头人听了笑了笑，　　　　　The headman listened smiling,
一句一句把话说：　　　　　Then spoke slowly:
"我当头人是莫米安的，　　"It was Momi's order for me to be your headman,
我按照莫米的主意办事，　　Which I followed accordingly.
日日夜夜把心都操碎了，　　I exerted all my efforts doing the job,
你们心里却不喜欢，　　　　Just to get your dislike and hatred.
现在自己栽田种地日子好过，Now I have a better life farming and planting,
我不愿当头人。"　　　　　I don't want to be your headman."

贝玛听了皱着眉头，　　　　The beima listened frowning,

十二奴局 // Twelve Nujus

一声一声把话说：	Then spoke clearly:
"我当贝玛也是莫米安的，	"It was also Momi's order for me to be your beima,
我按照莫米的主意办事，	Which I followed accordingly.
天天驱鬼治病忙得头昏眼花，	I was frantically busy evicting ghosts and healing people,
你们心里却嫌我，	Just to get resentment from your heart.
这样的贝玛，	A beima of this kind
我一天也不会当。"	Is not for me, not even for a day."

工匠听了眨眨眼，　　　　　　Hearing the words the artisan blinked,
一言一言把话说：　　　　　　And spoke distinctively:
　"我当工匠也是莫米安的，　　"It was also Momi's order for me to be your artisan,
　我按照莫米的主意办事，　　　Which I followed accordingly.
　天天打铁盖房累得我吃睡不安，I was so exhausted iron-making and house-building,
　你们心里却恨我，　　　　　　Just to get hatred from your heart.
　这样的工匠，　　　　　　　　An artisan of this kind
　我一天也不当。"　　　　　　Is not for me, not even for a day."

人们一起跪在地上，　　　　　　The people all knelt down,
流着眼泪苦苦哀求说：　　　　　Begging in tears:
　"尊敬的头人、贝玛和工匠，　"Honored headman, beima and artisan,
　我们没有你们活不成，　　　　We cannot live without you.
　要是你们不回去，　　　　　　If you do not come back,
　我们就跪在这里死也不起来。" We will stay on our knees here until death."

阿匹松阿
Apisong'a

头人的眼泪淌出来了，	The headman was all tears,
贝玛的鼻涕流出来了，	The beima was deeply moved,
工匠的声音哭出来了，	The artisan cried out loud,
三弟兄跟着人们回来了。	So they came back with the crowd.

头人回来了，
天天忙着给人们断事。
不听话的人拿棍子打，
恶人拿刀杀。
大家都规规矩矩过日子，
地方很快平定了。

When the headman was back,
He got busy settling disputes.
Naughty ones were spanked with sticks,
While the wicked was killed with swords.
Everybody obeyed the laws,
And the place was back to order.

贝玛回来了，
天天忙着给人们驱鬼治病，
寨门挂上了黄泡刺，
路口撒上了灶窝灰。
魔鬼不敢闯进寨子了，
人们平平安安过日子。

When the beima was back,
He got busy evicting ghosts and healing people.
Yellow rubus thorns were hung up at the gate,
And stove ash was cast on the road.
The devils dared not break into the village,
And people thus lived in ease and peace.

工匠回来了，
天天忙着给人们打铁盖房子。
锄头斧子和砍刀打出来了，
人们欢欢喜喜栽田种地。

When the artisan was back,
He got busy iron-forging and house-building.
Hoes, axes and machetes were forged,
And people farmed their land in joy.

新新的房子盖起来了，　　As new houses were built,
人们舒舒服服地安家。　　People settled down comfortably.
众：萨—萨！　　　　　　Chorus: Sah-Sah!

觉麻普德
Juema Pude*

---

* 觉麻普德：即觉麻建寨的意思。
  Pude means "to build a village".

十二奴局 // Twelve Nujus

萨啦阿依——	Sala Ayi–
远古的哈尼师厄[①]，	In the ancient Hanishi'e place
住着一家三个弟兄：	Lived three brothers:
大哥叫觉麻，	The oldest was named Juema
二哥叫觉车，	The middle one, Jueche
三弟叫觉冲。	And the youngest, Juechong.
这里森林密得望不见天，	The forest was densely shaded,
一年四季云雾腾腾，	And misty all year round.
野兽像蚂蚁一样多，	Wild beasts were crowded like ants,
毒虫像树叶一样旺，	And venomous insects abounded like leaves.
兄弟三人无法安身。	Days were hard for the brothers.
他们听说遥远的地方，	They heard that far away,
有块富饶的土地，	There was a piece of fertile land,
生出来的儿子力气大，	Where boys were born with strength,
生出来的姑娘样子俏；	And girls with pretty faces;
土肥水好好栽田和地，	Good soil and water were ideal for farming,
栽一年能吃两年；	That one year's work yielded two years' food;
芋头叶子比簸箕大，	Taro leaves were larger than dustpans,
一蓬嫩草够七头牛吃。	And a patch of grass was enough to feed seven cows.

---

① 哈尼师厄：古地名。

觉麻普德
Juema Pude

弟兄三个离开森林，	So the brothers left the forest,
去寻找这个好地方。	In search of this good place.
弟兄三人走了九天九夜，	Nine days and nights they had walked,
来到了一个河坝。	Before reaching a river basin.

河坝的谷米一年两熟， Corn here was harvested twice a year,
河坝的泉水四季流淌。 While spring water gushed all year long.
可是吃了谷米发瘴气， But the corn brought miasma disease,
喝了泉水肚子疼， And the spring water, stomachaches.
指甲壳上看不见血色， People had bloodless fingernails,
人的脸上没有亮光。 And their faces were ghastly pale.

他们认出这里不是好地方， Realizing it was a bad place,
又离开河坝去寻找。 They left for a better one.
他们又走了九天九夜， Nine days and nights they walked,
来到一块平地。 Before reaching a flatland.

这里的山四季常青， Here mountains were evergreen,
这里的水天天流淌。 And rivers flowed year round;
热风吹来给人营养， Warm air brought along nourishment,
凉风吹来人有血色。 And cool air, the breeze of life.

大哥觉麻停下来， Juema the oldest stopped,

十二奴局 // Twelve Nujus

忙对两个弟弟说：	Talking to his brothers:
"这里是个好地方，	"This is a nice place for farming,
水好土肥好栽田地，	With good soil and water.
我们停下来吧，	Let's just stop here,
再好好选个寨址安家。"	And find a good site to settle down."
觉麻三弟兄停下来了，	Juema and his two brothers stayed.
择了个吉祥的日子，	On an auspicious day,
登上一座高高的山顶，	They climbed up the top of a high hill,
去选一个安居乐业的寨址。	To choose an accommodating site for their village.
觉麻在山顶转去转来，	Juema paced around the hilltop,
眼睛朝四周的山梁望去：	Overlooking the ridges:
一条弯弯的河边上，	Along a winding river,
有一道歇着白云的梁子，	There was a ridge where clouds rest;
梁子上森林密密麻麻，	Across the ridge there was a dense forest,
森林中间有块洼地，	With a low-lying land in the middle;
洼地里清澈的龙潭，	The clear pond in the land
像一块明亮的镜子。	Was bright and shiny as a mirror.
觉麻高兴了，	Juema was glad,
觉麻看上了：	As he was into this place:
"这里是个好地方，	"This is a nice place,
这里是个好寨址，	Which makes an ideal site.

觉麻普德
Juema Pude

我们在这里建寨,	We will build our village here.
我们在这里安家。"	We will settle down here."

觉麻择了个最吉利的日子, On a most auspicious day,
带着两个弟弟, Juema and his two brothers,
抬着斧子和锯子, Carrying axes and saws,
到山上挑选柱子。 Went to the hill to choose pillars.

雷打过的树不能要, Thunderstruck trees were to be rejected,
要了房子容易着火烧; With which houses burned easily.
秃了顶的树不能要, Trees with no leaves were to be rejected,
要了子孙后代不会发; Which kept offspring from thriving.
虫吃过的树不能要, Worm-damaged trees were to be rejected,
要了人会疾病多; Which caused various diseases.
空心的树不能要, Hollow trees were to be rejected,
要了房子盖得不稳扎。 Which made shoddy houses.

先到东边山上找, They searched first in the east of the hill,
整个山林瞧过了, Where the whole forest was inspected.
挑过去挑过来, At great length,
挑过了林中所有的树木, All trees were checked in the forest,
没有一棵如意的树, But no one was to their liking,
没有一棵合心的树。 No one was satisfying enough.

来到北边山上找，	They searched then in the north of the hill,
转遍了整个山林，	Where the whole forest was inspected.
挑过去挑过来，	At great length,
挑过了林中所有的树木，	All trees were checked in the forest,
没有一棵如意的树，	But none was to their liking,
没有一棵合心的树。	None was satisfactory.
来到西边山上找，	They went to search in the west,
转遍了整个山林，	Where the whole forest was inspected.
挑过去挑过来，	At great length,
挑过了林中所有的树木，	All trees were checked in the forest,
没有一棵如意的树，	But none was to their liking,
没有一棵合心的树。	None was satisfactory.
来到南边山上找，	They searched in the south of the hill,
转遍了整个山林，	Where the whole forest was inspected.
挑过去挑过来，	At great length,
挑过了林中所有的树木，	All trees were checked in the forest.
在一个朝阳的山坡上，	Finally on a sunny hillside,
砍到了坚硬标直的栗木柱。	A sturdy and upright chestnut tree was cut down.
择了个吉祥的日子，	On a most auspicious day,
到河边的山坡上割茅草。	They went to collect grass on the hillside.
做过雀窝的茅草不能要，	Grass in the bird nests was to be rejected,

觉麻普德
Juema Pude

要了麻蛇会进家里来；	Which would attract snakes into houses;
蛆虫吃过的茅草不能要，	Grass once eaten by grubs was to be rejected,
要了耗子会来做窝；	Which would attract rats to build nests;
绿茵茵的茅草不能要，	Fresh green grass was to be rejected,
要了雨天会漏雨；	Through which rain would seep;
倒在地上的茅草不能要，	Grass lying on the ground was to be rejected;
要了风天不挡风。	Which could not keep out the wind.

转来转去地找， They searched around,
挑来挑去地选， Being careful and picky.
找遍了山山岭岭， Every mountain had been explored,
踩遍了沟沟洼洼， And every marsh land treaded.
在一面朝阳的山坡上， Finally on a sunny hillside,
割到了黄生生的茅草。 Yellow grass was collected.

择了个吉祥的日子， On a most auspicious day,
到箐沟割藤子。 They went to cut vines near the creek.
鬼藤子①不能要， Ghost vines① were to be rejected,
要了容易引鬼进家来； Which would attract ghosts into houses.
蛆虫吃过的藤子不能要， Vines once eaten by grubs were rejected,
要了地神不喜欢； Which was to the dislike of the god of land.
发出来的嫩藤子不能要， Tender vines were to be ruled out,
要了扎不稳竹排； Which could not bind the bamboo rafts tight;

---

① 鬼藤子：即血藤。

① Bloodvines.

十二奴局 // Twelve Nujus

挂着蛇蜕皮的藤子不能要，	Vines with snake skins on them were to be ruled out,
要了会吓着祖宗。	Which would scare ancestors away.
转来转去地找，	They searched around,
挑来挑去地选，	Being careful and picky.
钻遍了每一条箐沟，	Every brook had been explored,
找遍了每一条冲冲，	And every creek treaded.
在一条深深的箐沟里，	Finally in a deep brook,
割到了牢牢的藤子。	They cut down tough vines.
择了个吉祥的日子，	On a most auspicious day,
到山坡上砍竹子。	They went to cut bamboo on the hillside.
做过蜂窝的竹子不能要，	Bamboo used to nest bees was to be rejected,
要了容易引豹子进家来；	Which attracted leopards into the house;
断了尖尖的竹子不能要，	Bamboo with their tips gone was to be rejected,
要了人命活不长；	Which was an omen of short lives;
开花的竹子不能要，	Flowering bamboo was to be rejected,
要了要败家产；	Which indicated the loss of family property;
蛆虫吃过的竹子不能要，	Bamboo once eaten by grubs was to be rejected,
要了人容易生疮。	Which was likely to cause ulcers.
转来转去地找，	They searched around,
挑来挑去地选，	Being careful and picky.
找遍了每一蓬竹子，	Every grove of bamboo had been explored,

觉麻普德
Juema Pude

踩遍了每一片竹林，	And every bamboo forest treaded.
在朝阳的山坡上，	Finally on a sunny hillside,
砍到了俏生生的竹子。	Handsome bamboo was chopped down.

择了个吉祥的日子，　　　　On a most auspicious day,
找块平地脱土基。　　　　　They went to find soil to make the base.
黑土不能要，　　　　　　　Black soil was to be rejected,
用黑土打出来的土基不方正；With which the base would go askew.
白土不能要，　　　　　　　White clay was to be ruled out,
用白土打出来的土基不牢靠；With which the base would be shaky.
夹石子的土不能要，　　　　Soil mixed with gravel was to be rejected,
用夹石子土打出来的土基容易裂。With which the base would crack easily.

转来转去地找，　　　　　　They searched around,
挑来挑去地选，　　　　　　Being careful and picky.
踩遍了每一个山坡，　　　　Every slope had been treaded,
找遍了每一个冲沟，　　　　And every gully explored.
在山脚的洼地上，　　　　　Finally in the depression by the foot of the hill,
找到打土基的红土。　　　　Red base-building soil was found.

择了个吉祥的日子，　　　　On a most auspicious day,
选个牢固的地基。　　　　　They went to find a proper foundation.
有洞的地基不能要，　　　　Foundations with hollow cores were to be rejected,
要了雨天房子会坍塌；　　　On which houses would collapse on rainy days;

十二奴局 // Twelve Nujus

走动的地基不能要,	Moving foundations were to be rejected,
要了以后房子会梭倒;	On which houses would crumble;
垭口上的地基不能要,	Foundations in the mountain gap were to be rejected,
要了房子会被风吹掉;	On which houses were easily blown away;
冲沟沟里的地基不能要,	Foundations in the gully were to be ruled out,
要了雨天会被洪水淹。	Which would be flooded on rainy days.
转来转去地找,	They searched around,
挑来挑去地选,	Being careful and picky.
找遍了每一块土块,	Every piece of clod had been explored,
踩遍了每一道坷坎,	And every bumpy road treaded.
在一块朝阳的山坡上,	Finally on a sunny hillside,
选好了牢固的地基。	They made their choice of a solid foundation.
地基踩好了,	So the foundation was found,
地基选定了。	The foundation was chosen.
杀只大红公鸡祭天地,	They killed one rooster to sacrifice,
求天神地神保佑平安。	Praying for blessings from the gods.
挖去松软的浮土,	The soft surface soil was removed,
平出平坦的地基。	And the foundation leveled.
柱子砍来了,	With the pillars they cut,
茅草割来了,	The grass they collected,
藤子扯来了,	The vines they ripped off,

觉麻普德
Juema Pude

竹子砍来了，	The bamboo they chopped,
土基打好了，	The soil base they built,
地基平好了，	The foundation they leveled,
要立柱子啰，	They were ready to erect the pillars,
要盖房子啰。	As well as build the house.

择了最好的日子立柱子，　　Pillars were erected on the best day,
三个弟兄一起砌土基，　　　When the three brothers laid the soil base,
三个弟兄一起拴椽子，　　　Fastened the rafters,
三个弟兄一起铺茅草。　　　And spread the grass.
新新的房子盖好了，　　　　In the brand new house,
立起三个石头做锅脚石，　　Three stones were put up as a stove,
拿来三把干干的柴火，　　　And three dried pieces of wood
燃着柴火暖和和，　　　　　Were kindled to start the fire.
灰蓝蓝的火烟升上天，　　　As gray smoke rose to the sky,
四面八方都知道这里安了寨子。People near and far knew of the village.
要使寨子有个好名声，　　　May the village have a good name,
让好名声传到遥远的地方。　Which would spread to the far distance.

房子盖好了，　　　　　　　Now the house was built,
要找个好好的水井。　　　　It was time to find a good well.
雨季才会冒水的龙潭不能要，Springs with seasonal water were to be rejected,
田地里滴下来的尾水不能要，So was the drainage water from the fields.
会冒浑水的龙潭不能要，　　Springs with muddy water were to be rejected,

— 103 —

十二奴局 // Twelve Nujus

遍地浸出来的水不能要。	So was the water covering the ground.
只要清清的龙潭水,	Only springs with clear water were acceptable,
龙潭水是龙吐出来的。	Which had been spit out by the dragon.

龙吐出来的清泉水,   The clear spring water spit by the dragon
甘甜清凉最养人的心。   Was sweet, refreshing and nourishing.
吃龙潭水长大的儿子,   Young men who grew up drinking the water
个个勤劳勇敢有本事;   Were all diligent, brave and capable;
吃龙潭水长大的姑娘,   Girls who grew up drinking the water
个个生得像花一样俏。   Were all as pretty as flowers.

转来转去地找,   They searched around,
挑来挑去地看,   Being careful and picky.
找遍了每一条冲冲,   Every gully had been explored,
踩遍了每一道山梁,   And every ridge treaded.
在寨边的洼地里,   Finally in the depression near the village,
找到了一眼清澈的龙潭。   They found a clear wellspring.

挖去旁边的泥土,   They removed the nearby soil,
抬来硬硬的石板,   And brought along hard slate.
把四周砌起来,   They built up walls around,
把龙潭围在中间。   With the wellspring in the middle.
水井修好了,   Now the well was built up,
杀一只红公鸡祭献天地,   They killed a rooster as a sacrifice,
求天神地神好好保护龙潭,   Begging the gods' protection,

觉麻普德
Juema Pude

一年四季都冒清清的泉水。	So they could have clear water all year round.

寨头封起一片林,
世世代代一个不要砍。
安一座普玛①做护寨神,
每年杀一次猪鸡敬献,
请求护寨神显灵,
保佑全寨人无灾无难,
保佑猪鸡不病不死,
保佑牛羊又肥又壮,
保佑年年风调雨顺,
保佑庄稼年年丰收。

A patch of forest was closed up near the village,
In which all the trees were to be protected.
A Puma① statue was established as the village god,
To whom sacrifices of pork and chickens would be offered yearly.
In return blessings were asked,
For villagers to be free from disasters,
And pigs and chickens from diseases;
Cattle and sheep to be fat and strong,
Weather to be favorable,
And bumper harvests celebrated year after year.

寨边的草坪上,
安作玩乐的磨秋②场。
砍来坚硬的栗木,
栽起永世不朽的磨秋桩。
每年六月矻扎③到了,
牵来肥壮的黄牛,

The lawn beside the village
Was allocated as the happy Moqiu② Square;
Hard chestnut wood was cut down,
To build an everlasting Moqiu Pole.
Every June when the Kuzha③ Festival came,
Strong cows would be killed

---

① 普玛:即护寨神。有的译为龙树,不确。
② 磨秋:哈尼族一种传统的文体器具。
③ 矻扎:哈尼族的一个传统节日。

① The village god of the Hani.
② Traditional Hani sport equipment.
③ A traditional Hani festival in June.

十二奴局 // Twelve Nujus

在磨秋场上杀翻；	On the Moqiu Square;
点亮松明火，	Torches would be lit,
门头挂上绿松枝，	And green pine branches hung on the doors;
男女老少敲锣打鼓，	People of all ages would beat drums and gongs,
迎接神仙威咀到寨上。	To welcome Weizui, the god to their village.

神仙威咀来了， On his arrival Weizui, brought the village
给寨子带来幸福和吉祥。 Happiness and good fortune.
神仙威咀骑着白马要走了， When Weizui, was about to leave on his white horse,
全寨男女老少到磨秋场， Villagers of all ages came to the Moqiu Square,
擂响地神听得见的牛皮鼓， Beating drums and gongs loud enough,
敲响天神听得见的锣铓， For the earthly and heavenly gods to hear.
跳起欢乐的鼓舞， They danced to the beat merrily,
骑着磨秋升到天上， And swung the Moqiu up into the sky.
欢送我们的神仙威咀， In this way Weizui was warmly sent off,
骑着白马回到遥远的地方。 Back home far away on his white horse.

庄稼收完了， After the harvest,
黄生生的谷子收回来了， When yellow millet was collected,
杀翻肥肥的大猪， Fat pigs were to be killed,
踩好白白的糯米粑粑， White glutinous rice cakes were to be made,
烧一甑香甜的焖锅酒， Sweet pots of liquor were to be stewed,
宰杀大大小小的鸡鸭。 Chickens and ducks were to be killed.

请天神来过新年， It was time to celebrate the New Year.

觉麻普德
Juema Pude

请地神来过新年；	Both heavenly and earthly gods were invited,
接回祖先来过年，	So were the ancestors,
接回和祖宗不在一起的家人①	And all the wandering spirits of the family①.
来过年；	In this way a new year started,
新的一年开始了，	When the family spent a few days together in joy.
一家人欢欢喜喜过几日。	

要盖寨门了， / Then it was time to build a gate for the village;
要给寨子安个大门了。 / It was time to get it installed.
抬来大大的石头， / With large stones
砍来坚硬的锥栗木， / And hard chestnut logs,
寨门盖好了， / The village gate was set up,
老人小娃有玩的地方了。 / Where both the elder and the young could have fun.

寨门盖好了， / As the gate was built up
寨门安好了， / And securely installed,
把客人请进寨子来， / Guests were invited into the village,
把恶人堵在寨门外。 / While the devils were blocked outside.

寨门盖好了， / As the gate was built up,
请来高能的贝玛， / The capable beima was asked
把寨里的魔鬼驱出寨门， / To expel all devils from the village,
把灾难和疾病赶出寨门； / Along with disasters and diseases.

---

① 指非正常死亡的人。

① The spirits of those who died unnaturally.

十二奴局 // Twelve Nujus

砍来黄泡刺，	Yellow bubble thorns were cut down,
稳稳挂在寨门上，	To be firmly hung up on the gate,
把魔鬼挡在寨门外，	To keep the devils away from the village,
把灾难和疾病挡在寨门外。	And disasters and diseases as well.
寨门盖好了，	With the gate built up,
寨子建起来了。	The village took shape gradually.
房前屋后要栽上树：	Trees were to be planted around the houses:
寨脚的田坝栽杨柳，	Willow trees along the basin,
寨脚的坡子上栽竹子，	Bamboo on the slope,
寨门外边栽大青树。	And banyan tress outside of the gate.
寨子栽上了树木，	Seeing the trees planted,
寨神心里老实喜欢，	The village god was very glad
天天守在寨子里。	To stay and look after the village.
寨子像大象筋拉着一样稳扎，	The village was stable as though tied to elephant tendons,
寨子像大象皮箍着一样牢固，	And firm as though reinforced by elephant skins.
寨里的房子不会歪倒了，	Houses in the village would remain upright,
寨脚的陡坡不会梭坍了。	And the steep slopes down from the village would never collapse.
觉麻三弟兄把寨建起来，	In this way Juema and his brothers
寨子的名字叫麻密①，	Built up the village named Mami.

---

① 麻密：寨名。

觉麻普德
Juema Pude

觉车到各地建街子， Then Jueche went around to hold fairs,
觉冲到别处建寨当首领， And Juechong set up villages in other places,
觉麻留在麻密寨安家创业。 While Juema settled down in Mami.
人一代一代繁衍， As people multiplied over generations,
世间的寨子一寨一寨建起来。 Villages multiplied one after another.
众：萨—萨！ Chorus: Sah-Sah!

牡实米戛
Mushimiga*

---

* 牡实米戛：即天血掉落在地上的意思，其意为生儿育女。
　Mushimiga means the blood of childbearing.

十二奴局 // Twelve Nujus

萨啦阿依——	Sala Ayi–
天上有滴红彤彤的血,	From the sky a huge drop of red blood
忽然掉下大地。	Suddenly fell to the earth.
血洒落在哪里?	Where did it land?
洒落在寨子边的草坪上。	It spilled on the lawn near the village.
猪啊,请你不要去拱土,	Oh pig, please refrain yourself
也不要去踏草坪。	From dirt-rooting and lawn-treading.
猪摇摇摆摆游出寨子,	But the pig staggered out of the village,
天上的血沾在猪身上了。	And got stained by the blood.
狗啊,请不要去咬猪,	Oh dog, please keep yourself
也不要乱叫。	From attacking and barking.
狗冲出寨子咬猪,	But the dog rushed out to bite the pig,
天上的血沾在狗毛上了。	And got stained by the blood.
女人啊,请不要去打狗,	Oh woman, please control yourself
也不要发躁。	From making a fuss about the dog.
女人骂着打狗,	But the woman hit the dog, swearing
天上的血又沾到女人身上了。	And got stained by the blood.
寨中有人说:	People talked in disapproval:

牡实米夏
Mushimiga

"狗血抹在人身上，　　　　　　"That dog's blood on your body
血糊哩啦多腥气，　　　　　　Appears so messy and stinky,
威咀看到不顺眼，　　　　　　Weizui will surely be offended.
还是赶快洗了吧！"　　　　　Just wash it away promptly!"

沾在人身上的血，　　　　　　The blood stain on the woman
红得像朵大红花，　　　　　　Was as crimson as a hibiscus flower.
那不是猪血，　　　　　　　　It was neither pig's blood
那不是狗血，　　　　　　　　Nor dog's blood,
是人要发展兴旺的血。　　　　But the blood for humans to thrive.

不是黑头鸪尾下的毛发红，　　What was shining was not the red tail of the black
是女人身上流出的血红亮；　　　　　partridge,
不是园子里的桃子开花，　　　But the blood from the women.
是血在女人们的身上开花。　　What was blooming was not the garden peach tree,
　　　　　　　　　　　　　　But the blood from the women.

不会开花结果的树不要栽，　　Fruitless trees are to be discarded,
能开花结果的树人喜欢；　　　While productive trees are always cherished.
果实累累的桃树人爱护，　　　Just as fruitful peach trees are tenderly loved,
会生儿育女的女人才值钱。　　Women that can have children are valuable.

我家的女人，　　　　　　　　The woman in my house
不像别人一样，　　　　　　　Was quite different from others.

十二奴局 // Twelve Nujus

身子发冷发热，	Fever and chills went through her,
脚瘫手软没有力气。	Making her too weak to move her arms and legs.
走路跟不上人家，	She lagged behind while walking with others,
喘气不同别人，	And was always short of breath.
吃饭没有滋味，	She tasted nothing when eating,
喝水也不清甜，	And felt nothing when drinking water.
上山下田不爱做活计，	Disinterested in any farm labor,
一天到晚没有精神，	She was low-spirited all day long;
她不是生病软绵绵，	It's not illness that made her weak,
是肚子里怀娃娃了。	But that she had a baby inside her.
娃娃怀两个月了，	Two months into the pregnancy,
一只手一只脚长出来了；	The baby had one hand and one foot formed;
娃娃怀三个月了，	Three months into the pregnancy,
两只脚一只手长出来了；	The baby had two feet and one hand formed;
娃娃怀四个月了，	Four months into the pregnancy,
两只脚两只手长出来了……	The baby had both two feet and two hands formed…
娃娃怀了九个月，	Nine months into the pregnancy,
像到时的花朵要谢，	Like a flower at its time to wither,
像成熟的瓜果要落，	Or a ripened fruit to fall,
生娃娃的月份到了。	It was the time for the baby to be born.
娃娃生出来了，	Then the baby came to the world,
下地会哭三声了，	With three loud cries;

牡实米夏
Mushimiga

脐带要割断下来了，	The umbilical cord was to be cut off,
娃娃不能给冷着，	And the baby to be kept warm.
阿爹三天不要出门下田，	For three days the father would stay home,
阿妈三天不要烧火煮饭。	And the mother would be spared of cooking.

生下一个孩子，
一家人都很高兴，
要煮糯米饭，
送给寨里的长老乡亲。

Now that a baby was born,
The whole family was very happy.
They would cook glutinous rice,
And present it to the elders in the village.

杀只鸡取个名字，
给男孩取的名字，
要同阿爸名字连着叫；
给女孩取的名字，
不兴同阿爸连着叫，
愿的是孩子能平安长大。

A rooster would be killed for child-naming;
The name for a boy
Was to be based on his father's[①];
While a girl's name,
Had nothing to do with her father's.
So the baby would grow up safe and sound.

抱在大腿上，
孩子会笑了，
会认阿妈了，
会认阿爸了，
像小山雀一样会叫了，

Held on the lap,
The baby laughed,
And recognized his mother,
As well as his father;
He began giggling like a tit,

---

① The Hani adopt a patronymic linkage system in naming males. —Translator's note

十二奴局 // Twelve Nujus

像小瓦雀一样会说话了。	And babbling like a sparrow.
在地上会爬着玩了，	Then he crawled on the ground playing,
摇摇晃晃地会走路了，	Learned to walk, staggering,
渐渐地会玩灰了；	And began playing with dirt;
一天一天地长大，	He grew up day by day,
像竹子一节一节升高，	Like bamboo trees developing new segments;
背着鸭笼会到寨脚放鸭子了，	He learned to walk ducks with a cage on his back,
别着镰刀会上山放牛了，	Graze cattle with a scythe hung on his hip,
唱着山歌会挖田了。	And plow the field while singing.
众：萨—萨！	Chorus : Sah-Sah!

杜达纳嘎
Duda'naga*

---

* 杜达纳嘎：即哈尼先祖迁徙歌。
  Duda'naga means songs of migration.

十二奴局 // Twelve Nujus

萨啦阿依——	Sala Ayi–
哈尼人最先在哪个地方？	Where did the Hani people first live?
后来为哪样又要搬迁？	For what reasons were they relocated?
前前后后在哪些地方栽过磨秋桩？	At what places did they install Moqiu poles?
是哪个先祖，	Which one of the ancestors
给我们找到了这可爱的家乡？	Found us this lovely homeland?

一 / I

萨啦阿依——
在那遥远的地方，
有一条宽阔的大江，
淌着金子一样的水，
闪烁着耀眼的金光。
江畔有块宽宽的平地，
是个美丽富饶的地方，
这块土地，
是哈尼阿甫①最先生活的家乡。

最古的时候，
哈尼祖先没有住的地方，

Sala Ayi–
In the far distance,
There was a wide river,
Where gold-like water flowed,
Glittering golden light.
On the bank there was a wide flat land,
Which was beautiful and fertile.
This land
Was the first home of the Hani Afu①.

In ancient times,
The Hani ancestors did not have a shelter.

---

① 阿甫：即先祖。

① Ancestors.

杜达纳嘎
Duda'naga

像猴子一样到处跑，	They drifted about like monkeys,
一天在一个地方。	Never staying in the same place more than one day;
不知过了多少年，	After many years,
不知换了多少代，	And many generations,
哈尼的祖先，	The Hani ancestors
养起了猪鸡牛羊，	Started raising livestock.
吆着猪鸡到处走，	They herded pigs and chickens,
吆着牛羊到处放。	And grazed cattle and sheep.
哈尼吆着猪和鸡，	Herding pigs and chickens,
吆着成群的牛羊，	Grazing cattle and sheep,
来到诺玛阿美①。	The Hani came to Nuoma'amei①.
诺玛阿美是个好地方，	Nuoma'amei was a nice place,
哈尼先祖看上了，	Which caught the Hani's eyes,
哈尼先祖喜欢了。	And took their fancy.
砍来直直的木头作柱子，	They cut down straight logs as pillars,
砍来长长的木头作大梁，	And long logs as the beams.
割来茅草和藤子，	With collected thatch and vines,
盖起了新新的草房。	They built brand new thatched cottages,
一边住人堆谷子，	Where people slept amidst the heaps of grain,
一边关猪养牛羊。	Sharing the space with pigs and cattle.

---

① 诺玛阿美：古地名，在今凉山彝族自治州西昌一带。

① An ancient place.

十二奴局 // Twelve Nujus

选寨头的大树做普玛①,	They chose a towering tree as Puma①
选寨边的毛木树做龙主②,	A Guger tree as Longzhu②,
选寨脚的草坪作磨秋场。	And the lawn down from the village as Moqiu Square.
杀猪祭普玛,	Pigs were killed and offered to Puma,
杀狗鸡祭龙主,	Dogs and chickens to Longzhu,
杀牛祭磨秋桩。	And cattle to the Moqiu Pole.
求天神和地神,	Gods from both heaven and earth
压邪除魔排灾难,	Were prayed to in order to ward off evil,
保佑全寨人平安,	Keep the whole village safe,
保障庄稼无灾害,	Protect the crops from being ruined,
保佑六畜肥又壮。	And bless all the domestic animals to thrive.
淌着金水的江畔,	Along the glittering river,
美丽富饶的诺玛阿美,	In the fertile land of Nuoma'amei,
庄稼长得好,	Crops grew very well,
栽出来的米饭特别香;	Yielding appetizing rice;
养的猪鸡,	Domestic pigs and chickens
多得像山上的雀鸟一样;	Abounded like birds in the hills;
养的牛羊,	Domestic cattle and sheep
多得像搬家的蚂蚁一样。	Were as countless as a marching army of ants.
金色的水,	The golden water

---

① 普玛：即护寨神。
② 龙主：即压邪除魔树。

① Puma: The village god of the Hani.
② Longzhu: Sacred Tree that can exorcise demons.

杜达纳嘎
Duda'naga

把世代的哈尼人哺养：	Nourished generations of Hani people:
吃金水长大的儿子，	Young men who grew up drinking it
个个是英俊勇敢的好汉；	All turned into handsome and courageous heroes;
吃金水长大的女儿，	Girls who grew up drinking it
个个是聪明美丽的姑娘。	All turned into smart beauties.
富饶美丽的诺玛阿美，	The rich and beautiful Nuoma'amei
哈尼人好吃好在的地方，	Was where the Hani enjoyed their lives.
每一寸土地，	Every inch of land
浸透着哈尼人的血和汗，	Was soaked with their blood and sweat;
每一棵草木是哈尼先祖的命根子，	Each plant was precious
这里是哈尼先祖安居乐业的天堂。	In this paradise where they lived happily.
熟透的甜果子，	Sweet ripe fruits
容易招来馋嘴的雀鸟；	Drew greedy birds easily;
肥壮的牛羊，	Fat cattle and sheep
会招来凶恶的豺狼；	Attracted ferocious wolves;
美丽富饶的诺玛阿美，	The fertile land of Nuoma'amei
招来了恶人的魔掌。	Risked the clutches of the evil spirits,
虎豹一样凶恶的恶人来了，	Who, wicked as tiger and leopard,
灾难降到哈尼人的头上。	Brought disaster to the Hani people.
恶人骑着大马，	The evil spirits came riding horses,
手里的长刀闪着寒光，	Swords in their hands glistening chilly light;

身上披着弓箭，	Bows and arrows on their back,
恶狠狠地闯进哈尼人的家乡。	They broke into the Hani's homes savagely.
才发出来的嫩苗，	Tender sprouting seedlings
经不住寒霜摧残；	Could not stand the frost damage;
才刚发起来的哈尼人，	Newly established Hani people
难把闯进家乡的恶人抵挡。	Could hardly resist villains.
哈尼人的鲜血，	The Hani's blood
像河水一样流淌；	Was flowing like a river;
哈尼人的头颅，	The Hani's heads
像石头一样落在地上。	Fell to the ground like stones.
恶人抢走了金黄黄的谷子，	They were robbed of the golden millet,
赶走了成群的牛羊。	Flocks of cattle and sheep.
美丽的家园被践踏了，	As their beautiful homes were trampled,
无辜的哈尼人遭了祸殃。	The innocent Hani suffered.
亲亲的父老兄妹，	My dear elders and siblings,
恶人霸占了我们的家乡，	As villains have taken over our hometown,
吃住都不安宁了，	We can no longer enjoy our peaceful lives.
不能再忍受这样的灾难，	Such a disaster is too harsh to endure.
赶快背上东西，	We'd better bring our stuff along,
赶着成群的牛羊，	Herding our cattle and sheep,
牵扶年迈的老人，	Holding the old by their arms,
背上年幼的儿子姑娘，	Carrying young children on our backs,

杜达纳嘎
Duda'naga

大家一起走吧，

去找安居乐业的地方。

众：萨—萨！

And leave this place,

In search of a peaceful land.

Chorus: Sah-Sah!

二

II

萨啦阿依——

不知走了多少个白天，

不知过了多少个黑夜，

来到了一座高高的山上，

疲倦的人们停下来休息。

山脚下有个大海，

海边有个宽宽的坎子，

男女老少看见了，

心里有说不出的高兴。

Sala Ayi–

Countless days they had walked,

Countless nights they had traveled,

Before they reached a high mountain,

And stopped to take a rest, exhausted.

At the foot there lay a great lake,

And a broad field by its side.

The sight filled all people alike,

With unspeakable joy.

亲亲的父老兄妹，

我们找到了一块好土地。

这里叫洪阿[①]，

是个宽宽的坝子，

地平草嫩好养牛羊；

水好土肥好栽谷子。

大家停下来吧，

My dear elders and siblings,

We've found a good land.

The place is named Hong'a[①],

Which is a broad basin with good water and soil,

Ideal for animal-grazing,

And perfect for millet-growing.

Let's just stop here,

---

① 洪阿：据传即今昆明。

① Now it is called Kunming.

十二奴局 // Twelve Nujus

我们就在这里安寨子。	And build our village.
砍来了长长的大梁,	They chopped down long beams,
砍来了粗粗的柱子,	As well as thick pillars;
割来了黄黄的茅草,	They collected yellow thatch,
扯来了牢牢的藤子,	Together with firm vines;
筑起了厚厚的泥墙,	They built up thick mud walls,
盖起了新新的房子。	And constructed new houses.
普玛安起来了,	As the Puma Statue was set,
龙主建起来了,	The Longzhu decided,
磨秋桩也立起来了,	The Moqiu Pole installed,
水井挖好了,	And the well dug,
哈尼又安起了寨子,	The Hani had their village built,
赶起了热闹的街场,	And open markets crowded again.
男女老少欢欢喜喜。	All people were so joyful,
美丽的洪阿,	As beautiful Hong'a
成了哈尼人生活的土地。	Became their dwelling place.
富饶的洪阿,	The rich land of Hong'a,
哈尼生活的地方,	Where the Hani lived,
头人管得好,	Was well-managed by the headman,
整个地方平平安安;	So it was safe and peaceful;
贝玛背得好,	The beima hosted good rituals,

杜达纳嘎
Duda'naga

百姓没有灾和难；	So people were kept away from disaster.
工匠肯出力，	The artisan was willing to contribute,
寨子越来越繁荣兴旺。	So the village prospered day by day.

幸福的日子， When happy days
刚刚滋润了枯锈的心肠， Had just nourished the desperate hearts,
天大的灾难， Huge calamities
又降到哈尼人的头上： Once again fell upon the Hani:
恶人挥舞着长刀， The villains, waving long swords,
又闯到哈尼人的家乡。 Broke into their homeland.
受苦的哈尼人， The Hani who had suffered a lot
又遭到了恶人的摧残。 Once again were ravaged.

头人当不成官了， The headman was no longer able to rule,
地方乱得像火烧蜂窝； And the place was messy like a beehive on fire;
贝玛背不成了， The beima could no longer host rituals,
百姓多灾多难死亡多； And people suffered agony and many died;
工匠做不成活计， The artisan could no longer do his job,
寨子变成一片荒凉。 And the village was devastated.
可怜的哈尼人， The poor Hani
再也无法住在洪阿这地方。 Could no longer stay in Honga.

亲亲的父老兄妹， My dear elders and siblings,
恶人又闯到我们的家乡， The evil has broken into our homes again.

十二奴局 // Twelve Nujus

头人、贝玛和工匠，	The headman, the beima and the artisan,
受到恶人的摧残；	All are mistreated;
无辜的百姓，	Innocent people,
受尽了天大的灾难。	All are subjected to disaster.
赶快背上东西，	We'd better bring our stuff along,
赶快赶着成群的牛羊，	Herd our cattle and sheep,
牵扶年迈的老人，	Hold the old by their arms,
背上年幼的儿子姑娘，	Carry young children on our backs,
大家一起走吧，	And leave this place,
去找个安居乐业的地方。	In search of a peaceful land.
不知过了多少条江，	Countless rivers had been crossed,
不知过了多少条河，	Countless streams passed,
不知翻了多少座山，	Countless hills tramped over,
受苦的哈尼人哟，	Before the miserable Hani people
来到了窝你①地方。	Reached the basin of Woni①.
窝你坝子，	The basin of Woni
土地肥得像猪板油一样；	Had land as fertile as lard,
草有竹子粗，	Grass as thick as bamboo,
高高的杨柳树齐天长。	Tall willow trees reaching into the sky.
亲亲的父老兄妹，	My dear elders and siblings,
我们来到了窝你地方。	We've come to Woni.

---

① 窝你：即今开远。 ① Now it is called Kaiyuan.

杜达纳嘎
Duda'naga

窝你地平水又好，	Land flat and water clean,
是块黑油油的肥土壤。	Woni is a fertile place with its black soil,
水好土肥好栽谷子，	Ideal for millet-growing,
草旺地宽好养牛羊。	And perfect for cattle-grazing.
大家停下来吧，	Let's just stop here,
我们就在这里盖新房。	And build our new house here.
肥沃的窝你，	Thus fertile Woni
成了哈尼人的家乡。	Became the Hani's hometown.
栽一把秧能收一背谷子，	A handful of seedlings produced a basketful of millet,
田棚成了满满的谷仓；	And shacks were all turned into full barns;
半背谷子能踩一斗米，	A half basketful of millet made a peck of rice,
煮出来的米饭满坝子香。	Which, when cooked, filled the village with its aroma.
栽的棉花有大树高，	Cotton plants grew as high as trees,
结出的棉桃大得像顶草帽。	Bearing bolls the size of straw hats.
满坝盛开的棉花，	Cotton in full bloom all over the basin
像冬天的云海一样，	Was like a sea of clouds in the winter.
轧出的棉絮绒又绒，	With which fluffy fibers were made,
纺出的棉线细又长，	Before fine and long thread was spun out;
织出的布匹洁白柔软，	Then white soft cloth was woven,
哈尼人穿上了暖和和的衣裳。	And the Hani were clad with warm clothes.
泥鳅虽然香肥身子短，	The loaches were delicious but short,

十二奴局 // Twelve Nujus

幸福的日子过不长；	And happy days never last long;
可怜的哈尼人，	The poor Hani
又遭到了天大的祸殃。	Experienced a huge calamity again.
七天七夜下大雨，	Heavy rain lasted seven straight days and nights,
窝你坝子变成了汪洋。	Turning the basin of Woni into a sea.
洪水淹没了庄稼，	The flood drowned the crops,
洪水冲毁了新房。	And destroyed the new houses.
没吃没穿熬日子，	Deprived of food and clothing,
男女老少受尽了饥寒。	The Hani struggled with hunger and cold.
亲亲的父老兄妹，	My dear elders and siblings,
老天给我们带来了灾难，	God has brought us a disaster:
棉树变成了烂草，	The cotton plants have turned into rotten grass,
谷子陷进了泥塘。	While the millet is all stuck in the mud.
住在窝你，	Living in Woni,
大家都没心肠，	We've all lost our hearts.
大家一起走吧，	Let's just leave this place,
去找个安居乐业的地方。	In search of a peaceful land.
牵扶年迈的老人，	Holding the old by their arms,
背上年幼的儿子姑娘，	Carrying young children on their backs,
苦命的哈尼人，	The miserable Hani people
爬上坝子后面的大山，	Climbed up the hill behind,
男女老少不停息，	Without a moment of pause,

杜达纳嘎
Duda'naga

一直追赶落去的太阳。	In pursuit of the setting sun.
来到了一个宽阔的坝子，	They then arrived at a broad basin,
人们都叫它勒昂①，	Which was named Le'ang①;
到处长着黄饭花树，	Butterfly bush flowers were everywhere,
满坝飘着扑鼻的花香。	Filling the whole place with their scent;
恶心的臭气报凶恶，	Sickening odors were signs of evil,
醉人的花香报吉祥，	While the sweet scent of flowers suggested good luck.
男女老少，	People of all ages
都说勒昂是安居乐业的好地方。	Were sure that Le'ang was a good place to settle down.

男女老少齐动手，	They jointed their efforts,
在坝子中间盖起了新房。	To build new houses in the center of the basin.
宽阔的勒昂坝子，	Spacious Le'ang
成了哈尼人的家乡。	Thus became their hometown.
一块块的地开出来了，	Tracts of farmland were opened up,
撒上了玉米和高粱；	Where corn and sorghum seeds were scattered;
一丘丘的田开出来了，	Patches of paddg fields were cultivated,
栽上了绿茵茵的谷秧。	Where green rice seedlings were planted.

勒昂坝子，	The basin of Le'ang
是个好地方，	Proved to be a good place.
栽的庄稼得丰收，	Bumper harvests were always a sure thing,
猪鸡鹅鸭多得像蚂蚁，	Pigs and poultry were in large number like ants,

---

① 勒昂：即今建水。　① Now it is called Jianshui.

坝子里到处是肥壮的牛羊。	And herds of cows and sheep were seen everywhere.
吃鱼好像吃豆腐渣，	Fish were easily caught like Tofu residue,
香脆的牛干巴挂满房梁。	And crispy dried beef hung all over the beams.
头人管得好，	The headman ruled properly,
整个地方平平安安；	So it became a safe and peaceful place;
贝玛勤祭献，	The beima performed rituals frequently,
百姓没有灾和难；	So people were kept away from disaster;
工匠肯出力，	The artisan was willing to contribute,
寨子越来越繁荣兴旺。	So the village thrived day by day.
哈尼人的儿孙，	As the Hani population
一年比一年发展，	Expanded generation by generation,
人多勒昂坝子在不下，	Le'ang was too crowded to contain them all,
哈尼要到新的地方辟地盘。	So the Hani had to find new places.
亲亲的父老兄妹，	My dear elders and siblings,
我们的儿孙一天天发展，	As our families keep expanding,
再这样下去，	One day or another,
勒昂坝子会变成街场，	Le'ang would turn as crowded as a market
为了子孙后代，	For the sake of future generations,
我们去别处辟地盘。	We'd better go find other sites.
大家分头走吧，	Let's just go in separate groups,
各自去找自己的地盘。	In search of our own places.

杜达纳嘎
Duda'naga

勒昂坝子的哈尼人，	The Hani living in Le'ang
分成十二路去辟地盘：	Thus divided into twelve teams:
莫作带着朝东边走四路，	Four teams were led by Mozuo to explore the east,
去找安居的地方；	Where they could find a place to live;
区依带着朝南边走四路，	Four teams were led by Ouyi to explore the south,
去找乐业的地方；	Where they could do their jobs happily;
仰者带着朝西边走四路，	Four teams were led by Yangzhe to explore the west,
去找幸福的地方；	Where they could find happiness;
还有一部分	The remaining people
仍然留下来守勒昂。	Stayed behind in Le'ang.
众：萨—萨！	Chorus: Sah-Sah!

三 / III

萨啦阿依——	Sala Ayi–
有本事的仰者，	Yangzhe, the capable man,
我们的叶车祖先，	Ancestor of our Yeche branch,
带着父老兄妹，	Led his elders and siblings,
最后离开勒昂家园，	Left their home of Le'ang.
沿着西边的高山，	Along the mountain in the west,
一步不停地走向前。	They kept walking forward.
不知爬过了多少座山，	After countless mountains,
不知经历了多少艰难险阻，	Through hardships great and small,

十二奴局 // Twelve Nujus

勇敢的哈尼，	The brave Hani
来到一座高高的山巅；	Reached the top of a high hill,
看见山南有个宽宽的坝子，	Where they saw a broad basin in the south,
像个木盆放在群山中间。	Lying amidst the hills like a tub. |//

亲亲的父老兄妹， My dear elders and siblings,
平平的坝子就在眼前， Now we have a flat basin in front of us,
我们就到坝子里安家， Let's just settle down here.
我们就在坝子里栽秧， We can plant seedlings here,
世世代代， Where our children in the coming ages
就在坝子里过幸福的太平年。 Will be sure to enjoy their peaceful lives.

男女老少， People of all ages
来到波浪滔滔的元江边， Reached the surging river of Yuanjiang.
水深流急无法过， Stopped by the treacherous water,
望着平平的坝子急得打转转。 The Hani were at their wits' end pacing around.
聪明的仰者有主意， Smart Yangzhe came up with an idea,
用芭蕉树扎成筏子放在水中间， And bundled banana trees into a raft.
男女老少， People of all ages
坐着筏子渡过了天险。 Rode through this natural barrier on the raft.

这个坝子叫腊萨[①]， The basin was called Lasa[①],
夹在两条河中间。 Which lay between two rivers.

[①] 腊萨：即今元江。

[①] Now it is called Yuanjiang.

杜达纳嘎
Duda'naga

我们的祖先在此安了寨子，	Our ancestors set up their village here,
开出了一丘丘良田。	And opened up tracts of farmland,
栽出的谷子老实好，	On which grain grew extremely well,
栽出的甘蔗老实甜。	While sugar cane tasted very sweet.

有年腊萨发大水，　　　　　One year Lasa saw a big flood,
洪水愤怒地呼吼，　　　　　When raging water
河边的芦苇被冲走，　　　　Washed the reeds down to the lower level,
粗粗的芦根冲到了河下边。　And exposed the roots there.
住在河下游的异族人，　　　Aliens living downstream,
见到芦根烟筒般粗圆，　　　Seeing the roots as thick as their smoking pipes,
知道河头有块肥土地，　　　And learning of the existence of a rich land,
他们乐得笑眯了双眼。　　　Couldn't hold back their smiles.

洪水退去后，　　　　　　　As the flood receded,
一伙异族人顺河来到腊萨坝，A gang of aliens traveled upriver to Lasa,
像群苍蝇碰到了蜜，　　　　Just like a horde of flies attracted to honey.
借口来打鱼。　　　　　　　They, with the excuse of fishing,
久久赖着不肯把家还，　　　Stayed there for a long time.
不分白天黑夜，　　　　　　Days and nights,
一下不停地在坝子里头转。　They kept idling around in the village.

哈尼人安居乐业，　　　　　Seeing the happiness of the Hani,
异族人也想沾点边，　　　　The aliens wanted to steal some glory.

十二奴局 // Twelve Nujus

数不尽的人跑来寨子，	They flocked to ask with honeyed words
要求上门做姑爷的话比蜜甜。	To marry into the village.
先祖仰者心肠软，	Soft-hearted ancestor Yangzhe,
招下十个姑爷帮栽田。	Accepted ten of them as son-in-laws,
十个姑爷非常勤劳，	Who appeared very diligent,
一年到头不闲一天。	Never letting a day slip by without working.

十个姑爷来相伴，	With the company of their husbands,
十个姑娘干活日日跑在先；	The ten girls were highly motivated;
男女老少，	Men and women, the old and the young,
个个干活不愿闲。	Everyone did his job willingly.
人勤庄稼好，	Hard work paid off,
丰收一年接一年。	As good harvests came one year after another;
有吃有穿人兴旺，	The thriving family was well fed and clothed;
男女老少乐无边。	And the people all enjoyed their lives.

幸福日子没过多少年，	The happy days did not last long,
不幸的灾难驱赶哈尼人搬迁。	Before misfortunes drove the Hani away.
十个姑娘，	The ten girls,
听信了十个姑爷的蜜语甜言，	Hearing the sweet talk of their husbands,
叫来他们的公婆，	Brought their parents-in-laws,
带着异族的人到门前，	And other aliens along,
提出要分家，	Proposed to split the family,
要分财产和良田。	And take their share of the property.

杜达纳嘎
Duda'naga

先祖仰者不答应，	When refused by Yangzhe,
她们又哭又闹咒祖先。	They cried and cursed;
十个狠心的姑娘，	Their cruelty was like ten long knives,
像十把长刀戳在先祖的心间。	Stabbing into the heart of our ancestor.

先祖仰者， Our ancestor Yangzhe,
看出姑爷姑娘心里藏着奸， Seeing the ill intent of the ten couples,
心想分就分， Decided to do as they wished,
趁早割断祸水根源。 And cut the roots of trouble once and for all.
他把十个姑娘和姑爷， He called the ten couples together,
一起叫到了面前： And asked them of their plan:
"姑爷和姑娘， "My daughters and sons,
说说咋个分良田？" How should we split the farmland?"

狠毒狡猾的姑爷， The cunning and vicious son-in-laws,
不等姑娘张口先开言： Opened their mouths before their wives:
"亲亲的阿爸， "My dear dad,
我们只要一点点， We just want a little bit,
省得人去熬苦累， To save ourselves from hard labor.
叫只狗来踩分田， Let's bring a dog to do this job,
让狗走一圈， Walking him off the leash;
圈内就作我们的田。" The circle he makes will be our field."
先祖仰者不知是毒计， Yangzhe failed to see through the trick,
满口答应让狗踩分田。 And approved of the plan readily.

十二奴局 // Twelve Nujus

十个姑爷叫来只白狗，	The ten son-in-laws brought a white dog,
狗尾拴上蘸了油的破布片，	Strapping its tail with oil-soaked fabric,
破布片点着火，	On which they set fire,
吓得白狗叫着绕田坝蹿了一圈。	Scaring the dog to run wild in a wide circle.
全部良田都被姑爷分走了，	Thus all the fertile land fell into their hands,
上当的先祖仰者有苦难言。	And our ancestor had to suffer in silence.
全部好田被抢走，	As all the good fields were taken away,
哈尼人只好种剩下的一点瘦田。	The Hani had to make do with the poor soil.
异族人的心还不满足，	Yet the aliens were not contented,
故意把牛放到哈尼人的田中间，	Who went further to graze cattle on the Hani fields.
哈尼人的田埂被踩坏，	The Hani lands were trampled,
哈尼人的谷子被踏践。	And their crops ruined.
愤怒的先祖仰者，	In anger our ancestor Yangzhe,
砍断一条牛腿丢田边。	Cut off a cow leg and displayed it by the field.
狡猾的异族人，	The cunning aliens
来到先祖仰者的身边，	Came to visit Yangzhe,
装着低头来认罪，	And put on a look of regret,
认错的话说了一遍又一遍：	Saying they were sorry over and again:
"豹子抬剩的烂牛，	"It would serve these bad cattle right to be the leopards' prey!
糟蹋了好鲁鲁一片田，	
像这样谁见着都会气愤，	A good field ruined this way
砍断牛腿合大家心愿，	Certainly sparks indignation;

杜达纳嘎
Duda'naga

往后要是哪家牛来踩，	It speaks our minds to cut off the leg.
要比这回处罚更严。"	Should anybody dare to trespass in the future,
	More severe punishment will be applied."

毒蛇藏在绿草中，   Just like vipers hidden in the green grass,
笑脸掩盖着内心的阴险。   Deceitful hearts were covered by smiling faces.
我们的先祖仰者，   One day our ancestor Yangzhe
有天带着猎狗到山上转，   Walked his hound to the mountains.
回来的时候，   On his way back,
过着异族人抢占的那片地， He passed the field seized by the aliens.
狠毒的异族人，   The vicious aliens
很快把仰者围在中间：   Promptly surrounded Yangzhe in the middle:
"上次牛踩田，   "Last time when our cow trampled your field,
你砍了牛腿丢在田边，   You cut off its leg in the field.
牛是不懂道理的，   Although one can't talk sense into the beast,
可我们没有说一句怨言；   We accepted it without any complaint.
你是懂道理的人，   But you, a man of reason,
故意踩田毁我们的脸面，   Insult us by ruining our fields on purpose.
今天着砍你的腿，   Today we will cut off one of your legs,
丢到远远的坝子边。"   And throw it to the far side of the basin."

异族人举起闪亮的长刀，   Aliens raised shiny long swords,
哈尼人抬着磨快了的钩镰， While the Hani lifted sharpened sickles.
杀声埋葬了歌声，   Songs vanished amid the sound of fighting

十二奴局 // Twelve Nujus

鲜血染红了富饶的家园。	While blood reddened the fertile homeland.
异族人越打人越多，	More and more aliens joined the battle,
哈尼人越斗人越减。	While the Hani suffered the continuous loss of their peers.
受苦的哈尼人抵挡不住，	They could no longer resist the attack,
退到了腊萨坝子的东边。	And retreated to the east of the Lasa Basin.
我们的先祖仰者，	Our ancestor Yangzhe,
望着受苦的老少开了言：	Talked to his fellowmen in misery:

"亲亲的父老兄妹，   "My dear elders and siblings,
异族人多势众不怕天和地；   The aliens are fearless in crowds;
我们哈尼人少势力单，   We are at a disadvantage before them,
挨着异族的老牛鞭。   And that's why we got whipped.
从今以后子子孙孙要代代传：   All members should mark my words from now on:
哈尼人不得招姑爷，   Hani families will never take in son-in-laws;
出嫁的姑娘不得分田。   Married-off girls will have no share of the field.

"亲亲的父老兄妹，   "My dear elders and siblings,
仁慈的莫米不睁眼，   As merciful Momi keeps his eyes shut,
哈尼人受尽欺凌，   All the humiliation we've suffered
天神一点也看不见；   Is totally unknown to him;
十个姑娘是十把长刀，   The ten girls are like ten swords,
长刀戳烂了我的心田；   Which pierced my heart;
这样下去不得了，   We have to do something about it,

杜达纳嘎
Duda'naga

哈尼人的灾难越会增。	Or more disasters will fall on the Hani again.

"我们大家走吧,   "Let's just leave this place,
一个人的心也不要偏,   To save our hearts from going awry;
一个也不要落掉,   No one is to be left behind,
一个也不要逃潜。   Nor to run away.
顺河走下去,   Let's walk down the river,
一直走到出太阳的天边边,   To afar where the sun rises,
为我们的哈尼人,   For the sake of the Hani people,
寻找一个幸福的乐园。   In search of a happy paradise.

"我们的人多,   "We are great in number.
只要大家心齐,   As long as we are in one mind,
毒蛇不敢咬,   Vipers will be kept away,
魔鬼也不敢挨身边;   And devils will never come close;
老虎不敢来抬吃,   Tigers will not dare to eat us,
豹子也不敢来舔舔。   Nor will leopards come to have a bite.
放大胆子快走吧,   Let's just move with courage,
乐园就在遥远的前面。"   As paradise awaits us in the far distance."

苦命的哈尼人,   The miserable Hani,
流着悲伤的眼泪,   With tears of sorrow,
离开异族霸占的腊萨,   Left Lasa, the place occupied by aliens,
向遥远的东方搬迁。   And moved to the far east.

强壮的男人走前头，	Strong men walked in the front,
妇女老幼走中间。	Elders, women and children in the middle.
拿长刀的男人在前头开路，	Men with long swords cleared the path,
防卫的男人手持长矛跟在后边。	While those armed with spears guarded the rear.

白天大家出力赶路程，
晚上一群群老虎豹子扑到人跟前。
聪明的仰者主意高，
四周烧起大火防危险；
强壮的男人和猎狗睡边上，
女人和老幼睡在中间。
老虎豹子不敢来，
一群群躲进了森林里面。
众：萨—萨！

All walked on and on during the day,
But were in danger at night as beasts prowled around.
Smart Yangzhe got fantastic ideas,
Setting bonfires around to keep safe;
Strong men and hounds slept at the sides,
While the elders, women and children were in the center.
Tigers and leopards were kept away,
Hiding themselves inside the forest.
Chorus: Sah-Sah!

四 / IV

萨啦阿侬——
苦命的哈尼人，
我们叶车的老阿波①
不知过了多少个夜晚，

Sala Ayi–
The miserable Hani,
Ancestors of our Yeche branch,
Night after night,

---

① 阿波：即阿爷，这里指先祖的意思。

杜达纳嘎
Duda'naga

不知过了多少个白天；	Day after day,
不知爬过多少座山梁，	Had climbed countless ridges,
不知跨过多少条江河；	And crossed numerous rivers.
穿过无边无际的大坝子，	They passed through the vast basin,
一直顺着红河走到海边。	Down the Red River and reached a lake.

携带的粮食吃完了，　　　　They'd run out of food,
小娃娃们哭又叫，　　　　　Babies were crying, starved,
年迈的老人累又饿。　　　　The elders were tired and hungry.
我们的祖先仰者，　　　　　Our ancestor Yangzhe,
好比针尖戳心窝，　　　　　In pain as if having needles poke into his heart,
他站在海边上，　　　　　　Stood by the lake,
一句一句对大家说：　　　　And delivered a speech:

"亲亲的父老兄妹，　　　　"My dear elders and siblings,
幸福的乐园还没有找着，　　Despite our search for a happy paradise,
前面挡着无边的大海，　　　We are now blocked by the boundless lake.
没有吃的大家都挨饿。　　　Everybody is starving.
苦命的哈尼人，　　　　　　Miserable Hani people,
又遇到了灾祸。　　　　　　We are now in trouble again.
大家停下来吧，　　　　　　Let's just stop here,
在这里住上一些日子再说。"　And make plans after a few days' rest."

受苦的哈尼人，　　　　　　The Hani who had suffered a lot,

十二奴局 // Twelve Nujus

在海边平坝上住下来,	Settled at the land by the lake.
男人开田开地种庄稼,	Men opened up fields and grew crops,
女人拿鱼捞虾采野果。	While women fished and collected wild fruits.
有水不怕口干,	Thirsts were eased by water,
天气闷热不怕衣裳薄。	And thin clothes were enough in the hot weather.
没有办法了,	There's no other way left,
大家只能简简单单过生活。	But to lead a simple life.
海边的大坝子,	The basin by the lake
土地特别肥沃:	Turned out particularly fertile:
棉树要用斧子砍,	Cotton trees were to be cut down by axes,
谷秆可以做烟筒,	While grain straws were as thick as chimney;
高粱穗子如马尾,	Sorghum ears were in the shape of horsetails,
小米①穗子像雀窝。	And highland barley ears were like bird nests.
庄稼丰收了,	The Hani enjoyed a bumper harvest,
收得粮食万千箩。	Collecting grain in thousands of baskets.
可怜的哈尼人,	The poor Hani
一日两顿饭,	With two meals a day,
个个肚子饱,	All had their bellies full.
可是天气热得像火烧,	But the weather was so hot as if on fire,
老人小娃热死好几个。	Burning many elders and children to death.

---

① 小米:指一种稞类作物,并非指北方小米。

杜达纳嘎
Duda'naga

海边的大坝子，	The basin by the lake
再也没法生活。	Was no longer suitable for life.

"亲亲的父老兄妹， "My dear elders and siblings,
这里热得在不得， This place is too hot to endure,
大人早早就死去， Where adults die young
生下来的小娃不会活。 And babies are born dead.
这样在下去， If we continue living here,
我们会死得更多。 We will lose more people.
我们赶快走吧， We might as well leave soon,
过海去找幸福的乐园谋生活。" And seek a happy place across the lake."

我们的先祖仰者， Our ancestor Yangzhe,
肚子里的主意多。 Was a man of ideas.
派人找来木头和竹子， He had wood and bamboo collected,
扎成大大的筏子几十个， Which were bundled into dozens of rafts.
男女老少带上吃的东西， Men, women and children brought food,
一个筏子坐一伙。 And sat on the rafts in groups,
下海的筏子像簸米， Which were tossed by the sea
一直朝出太阳的地方簸。 Heading to where the sun rises.
老天突然扇扇子， Suddenly God flipped a fan,
蓝天顿时变成了大黑锅。 And the blue sky turned into a big black pot.
无边的大海摇晃起来， The boundless lake was shaken up,
遭了难的哈尼没法逃脱。 The tortured Hani saw no way out.

刮来一阵大黑风，	A gust of black wind
连筏带人被海水淹没。	Turned over the rafts and the passengers.
苦难的哈尼人，	The miserable Hani
又遭到了天大的殃祸。	Once again suffered a huge calamity.
不知过了多少个白天，	Many days had passed.
不知熬了多少个黑夜，	Many nights had gone by.
可怜的哈尼人，	The poor Hani
漂落在海边的沙滩上。	Drifted to the lake beach.
我们的先祖仰者，	Our ancestor Yangzhe,
被热热的太阳晒活。	Revived by the heat of the sun,
他爬起来四处去转，	Got up and turned around,
看看还有多少人活着。	To see how many survived.
他在沙滩上找了好几天，	He looked on the beach for several days,
好些人还是找不着。	But many were still missing.
找着的人里头，	Among those he found,
死掉的很多很多，	A great number were dead,
活着的男女老少总共只有百十个。	Leaving only dozens alive.
我们的先祖仰者，	Our ancestor Yangzhe,
带着大家去找地方谋生活。	Still had to find them a place to live in.
这里四处是平平的坝子，	There were flatlands around,
到处长满了大树和草根，	Where trees and grass roots grew.
没有一座齐天的高山，	There was no high mountain,

杜达纳嘎
Duda'naga

没有一条红河样大的江河；	Or any river the size of the Red River.
看不到一丝火烟，	No wisp of smoke was ever seen,
看不到一座村落。	No single village was visible.
走遍了四面八方，	The Hani explored in all directions,
四面八方都被大海围着。	Only to find the lake in the end.

我们的先祖仰者，
Our ancestor Yangzhe,

出来的时候对大家说：
Stepped out and said,

"亲亲的父老兄妹，
"My dear elders and siblings,

你们大家都看啰，
I want your attention.

这个没有人家的地方，
This unsettled place

四面八方都被大海围着，
Is surrounded by the lake.

狠心的恶人进不来，
Cruel villains could not force themselves in,

我们不消再遭殃祸。
So we are free from any calamity;

这是个好地方，
This is a nice place,

安个幸福的乐园蛮适合。
Quite fit for us as a happy paradise."

"太阳从东边出，
"The sun rises in the east,

慢慢又往西边落。
And sets slowly down in the west;

西边淌下来的红河水，
The Red River flows down from the west,

淌到东边的大海里汇合，
To merge in the lake at the east;

大海是水尾，
As the lake is where the river ends,

这地方就叫额咪① 啰。
Let's call this place Emi①.

---

① 额咪：即天边，水尾的意思。　　① The end of the river.

十二奴局 // Twelve Nujus

大家定下心来了,	We can settle down,
我们就在这里过生活。"	And have a happy life here."

受苦的哈尼人,	The Hani who had suffered a lot
在额咪安起寨子,	Set up their village in Emi.
盖起草房一间间,	Cottages were built one after another;
寨头建起了普玛一座,	With the Puma Statue built up;
寨边定了一座龙主林,	The Longzhu forest chosen;
寨中修了一口井,	A well dug out;
寨脚支起一棵磨秋桩,	The Moqiu Pole installed,
田地开出来了,	Farmland opened up,
男女老少心里热和和。	All villagers felt warm and cozy.

额咪是个好地方,	Emi turned out to be a nice place,
平平的土地老实肥沃:	With its flat fertile land:
棉树长得一间房子高,	Cotton trees grew as high as a house,
粗粗的谷秆能挂大秤砣。	And grain straws were as thick as scale beams.
庄稼年年长得好,	As crops grew well every year,
陈谷装满了筐筐箩箩;	Baskets were piled high with the past years' millet.
额咪家乡年成好,	Emi had seen harvest years one after another,
哈尼人日子过得乐呵呵。	And the Hani people enjoyed their lives contented.

额咪这地方虽说庄稼好,	Despite its fine crops,
瘴气却像魔鬼一样恶。	Emi was haunted by miasma.

杜达纳嘎
Duda'naga

瘴气熏得人们头晕眼花，	People got dizzy breathing,
喝了水后肚子好像胀破。	And had their bellies bloated drinking.
着了瘴气发起来，	When attacked by the miasma,
全身一下发冷一下又发热。	People had chills and fever.
哈尼人来到额咪九年，	In the nine years that the Hani dwelt here,
年年发瘴气死掉一些人。	Many people died of miasma.

我们的先祖仰者， Our ancestor Yangzhe,
年年都受瘴气折磨。 Was also tortured by miasma every year.
杀狗给他打瘴气， Dogs were killed for treatment,
吃了狗肉才得把命活。 Their meat saved him from death.
瘴气难断根， Yet the disease was ineradicable,
隔上一段时间又发作， Which came back once in a while.
虽然人没死， Although people did survive,
病得头发已全部掉落。 Their hair all fell off.

我们的先祖仰者， Our ancestor Yangzhe,
再也忍受不了瘴气的折磨， Could no longer live with the torture.
他望望西边天， He looked west,
痛心地对大家说： And talked in pain:
"亲亲的父老兄妹， "My dear elders and siblings,
这里的瘴气老实恶， This miasma is vicious,
这样下去会送掉命， And will kill us all one day.
还是回老家去算啰。" We'd better go back to our hometown."

十二奴局 // Twelve Nujus

乡亲们知道故乡好，
开始个个都听得心里乐。
可是想到故乡的恶人，
想到过去的灾祸，
想到归途中的风险，
异口同声对仰者说：
"回去九死一生太危险，
还是在额咪过过算啰。"

"大家不走就留下来，
安安心心在额咪生活，
我死也要回故乡，
不然我心里不安乐。"
仰者说完就开路，
坐着筏子离开额咪啰。
众：萨—萨！

五

萨啦阿依——
我们的先祖仰者，
坐着筏子渡大海，
鼓足全身的力气，

All missed their sweet home,
And were happy about the news.
But thinking of the wicked people there,
The calamities from the past,
And the risk on the way back,
They told Yangzhe in chorus:
"It's too dangerous to go back,
We would be better off staying here."

"If you choose not to leave,
Then just stay and enjoy your lives here.
I'm determined to go back,
Or I will never be happy."
With these words Yangzhe started off,
Leaving Emi on a raft.
Chorus: Sah-Sah!

V

Sala Ayi–
Our ancestor Yangzhe,
On his lake-crossing raft,
Spared no effort rowing,

杜达纳嘎
Duda'naga

拼命直朝西边天划。	Desperately towards the west.
老天突然扇扇子，	Suddenly God flipped a fan,
一阵大风把仰者吹到海边来。	And a gust of wind blew Yangzhe ashore.

仰者认出自己在红河口，　　　Finding himself at the end of the Red River,
高兴得立即把脚迈，　　　　　Yangzhe strode in ecstasy,
沿着红河一直往上爬，　　　　Along the river upstream,
走得比麂子还要快。　　　　　Faster even than a muntjac.
不知过了多少天，　　　　　　After countless days,
不知过了多少夜，　　　　　　And countless nights,
一个晴天的早晨，　　　　　　On a bright sunny morning,
来到腊萨下面的南洼①街。　　He arrived at Nanwa① street of Lasa.

我们的先祖仰者，　　　　　　Our ancestor Yangzhe,
没有自己的家和寨，　　　　　A man without a home,
没有落脚处，　　　　　　　　A man without a living place,
成了一朵飘游不定的云彩。　　Was then like a piece of wandering cloud.
有天赶南洼街，　　　　　　　One fair day in Nanwa,
仰者从别处转回来，　　　　　Where Yangzhe was wandering,
在那街场上，　　　　　　　　In happy surprise on that street,
见到岳父慈嘎哥欧乐开怀。　　He met his father-in-law Cigage'ou.
仰者诉说了承受的灾难，　　　Yangzhe told his life story of hardship,
岳父的眼泪挂满了两腮。　　　Which moved his audience to tears.

---

① 南洼：地名，在今元江县境内。　　① A place in today's Yuanjiang County.

十二奴局 // Twelve Nujus

善良的慈嘎哥欧	Kind-hearted Cigage'ou
把姑爷领回了自己的山寨。	Brought Yangzhe back to his village,
拿最好的东西给他吃,	Offering him the best food,
找来最好的药给他除病害,	And finding him the best medicine.
请来最高的贝玛,	The top-ranked beima was asked
把仰者的魂叫回来。	To summon the soul of Yangzhe back.
仰者的魂叫回来了,	As his soul was called back,
仰者的病慢慢好起来,	Yangzhe got well day after day;
黑黑的头发长出来了,	Black hair grew out,
疲倦的眼睛闪出了神采,	And dying eyes regained their glow.
出门走山路,	When he walked in the mountains,
比麂子还跑得快。	He was faster than the muntjac.
仰者的老婆在额咪死了,	Yangzhe' wife had died in Emi,
只是他一个人回来,	And he came back all the way alone;
差了个老婆,	Without a woman,
吃得再好日子也难挨。	Life was unbearable.
我们的先祖仰者,	Our ancestor Yangzhe,
要讨个老婆自己安寨。	Wanted to find a wife to settle down.
告别了善良的岳父,	Bidding goodbye to his kind father-in-law,
来到山高林密的江外①。	He came to the densely-forested south①.

---

① 江外：红河南岸俗称江外，北岸即江内。

① It refers to south of the Red River.

杜达纳嘎
Duda'naga

属马的日子，	On one Day of the Horse,
仰者来到热闹的马街，	Yangzhe came to the bustling fair,
转来转去想找个合心的老婆。	Looking for a suitable woman.
拥挤的街子中间，	In the crowded street,
红的绿的样样东西都卖，	Things of all colors were for sale,
但是街中间的女人，	But no single woman there
没有一张嘴使他感到可爱。	Appeared to have lips adorable enough for him.
转来转去地找，	He searched again and again,
转到街头钻过去钻过来。	First on the upper street.
热闹的街头，	It was lively and crowded,
吃的用的东西样样都有卖，	With all kinds of foods and tools for sale.
可惜在街头的女人，	But no single woman there
没有一张脸使他喜笑颜开。	Appeared to have a face to make him smile.
转来转去地找，	He searched again and again,
转到街尾钻过去钻过来。	Then on the lower street.
热闹的街尾，	It was lively and crowded,
穿的玩的东西样样都卖，	With all kinds of clothes and playthings for sale.
可惜在街尾的女人，	But no single woman there
没有一双眼睛给他带来欢快。	Appeared to have a pair of eyes to bring him joy.
先祖仰者，	Our ancestor Yangzhe
赶了马街赶羊街，	Went to the Sheep Fair after the Horse Fair.

十二奴局 // Twelve Nujus

跑遍了东西南北,	All directions were explored,
赶遍了所有的大街小街,	And all streets and lanes crossed,
合心的女人,	But a woman to his liking
一个也没有找得来。	Was nowhere to be found.

先祖仰者,	Our ancestor Yangzhe,
心灰失望地来到南洼街。	Came back to Nanwa Street disappointed.
刚走进街子,	The moment he set foot there,
一双迷人的眼睛使他发呆,	He was dazed by a pair of charming eyes,
高耸的胸脯使他高兴,	Thrilled by the plump breasts;
红润的脸庞使他非常喜爱。	And pleased by a rosy face.
仰者走过去细细一看,	Yangzhe walked over and looked carefully,
原来是小姨妹欧纽。	Just to find the owner to be his sister-in-law Ouniu.

仰者领着小姨妹,	Yangzhe took the hand of his sister-in-law,
走到岳父慈嘎哥欧的面前,	And went to his father-in-law Cigage'ou.
诉说找不到合心的老婆,	He poured out his trouble in finding a lovable wife,
请求再将欧纽嫁给他生后代。	And asked Ouniu to be married to him.
岳父同意了,	With the consent obtained,
仰者领着欧纽到米尼坎①安寨。	Yangzhe, with Ouniu, went to settle down in Minikan①.

不知过了多少年,	It was after so many days,

---

① 米尼坎:在今红河县境。　　① A place in today's Honghe County.

杜达纳嘎
Duda'naga

不知过了多少载，	So many years,
我们的先祖仰者，	That our ancestor Yangzhe,
终于得到了福气，	Finally got his blessing.
生了八个儿子，	Eight sons were born to him,
个个长得老实可爱。	All cute and adorable.

燕子飞去了十八回，　　Eighteen times the swallows had come and gone;
门前松树长了十八台，　Eighteen layers of growth the pine tree had left.
八个儿子长大了，　　　Now the eight sons were all grown-ups,
仰者将儿子一个个安排：Yangzhe reasoned to them one by one:
"我的儿们哟，　　　　 "My dear children,
请听我把道理说：　　　Please listen to my wisdom.
我们哈尼人，　　　　　We Hani people
经受了数不尽的灾难。　Have endured countless calamities.
平平的坝子虽然好，　　Flat basins are good,
天灾人祸太多我们不能在，But not for us as they may have disasters.
子子孙孙都不要到坝子安寨。Never shall our offspring settle in basins.

"高高的山梁，　　　　　"The high mountain ridges
山清水秀灾害少，　　　Are picturesque and peaceful.
山高不怕大水淹，　　　Floods will never happen on the mountains,
坡陡恶人很难爬上来，　And bad guys are kept away because of the steep slopes.
森林茂密难开路，　　　In the dense forest ways are hard to find,
坏人也不敢轻易进山寨，Villains could not easily force themselves into the village.

十二奴局 // Twelve Nujus

从今以后，	From this day on,
子子孙孙都在山上安寨。	All our children are to settle their homes uphill.

"亲亲的儿子们哟，　　　　　　　"My dear sons,
你们要牢牢记在心上：　　　　　　You must keep in mind:
诺玛阿美是我们的故乡，　　　　　Nuoma'amei is our hometown,
宽宽的坝子洪阿是我们的老寨，　　And the broad basin Hong'a is where we started;
窝你、勒昂、腊萨坝子我们在过，　We left traces in Woni, Le'ang, Lasa,
出太阳的额咪地方便有我们的
　　子孙后代，　　　　　　　　And our blood can be found in Emi where the sun rises.
还有在勒昂分开走了十二路，　　　Le'ang saw the division of twelve branches,
东南西北处处有我们哈尼人。　　　Which resulted in the spread of Hani in all directions.
切莫忘记了，　　　　　　　　　　You shall always keep this in mind,
往后有机会要认祖宗互相往来。" And resume close relations if the time comes."

天下的哈尼人哟，　　　　　　　　Hani people all over the world,
没有先祖就没有我们这一代。　　　Our ancestor is the reason we are here.
先祖的话做得药，　　　　　　　　His words are wise counsel,
子子孙孙要牢记在心。　　　　　　Which should be kept in mind.
断根的松树要枯死，　　　　　　　Just as pines will die with broken roots,
忘了祖宗的人活在世上不光彩。　　Those who forget their origins will live in disgrace.
亲亲的父老兄妹，　　　　　　　　My dear elders and siblings,
走到哪里都不要忘记祖宗和后代。　Never forget your past and future wherever you go.
众：萨—萨！　　　　　　　　　　Chorus: Sah-Sah!

汪咀达玛
Wangzuidama*

---

* 汪咀达玛：孝敬父母之称。
  Wangzuidama means filial piety.

十二奴局 // Twelve Nujus

萨啦阿依——	Sala Ayi–
天上的星星，	The stars in the sky
是太阳月亮生成的；	Are children of the sun and the moon;
地上的大树，	The trees on the ground
是种子长出来的；	Start from tender seeds;
世间的男男女女，	Men and women of this world
是阿爸阿妈生养成的。	Are born and raised by their parents.
爸妈生儿育女，	The process of child-raising
不像摘多衣果一样容易，	Is not as easy as fruit-picking,
不像撒荞子地一样省力；	Or as effortless as wheat-seeding.
花费的心血像流水一样多，	It takes rivers of blood and sweat,
使出的力气秤难称。	And effort that is hard to be weighed.
世间的儿和女，	Men and women in this world
爸妈的恩情重如山，	Owe much to their parents,
要时时刻刻记在心里。	Which should be kept in mind all the time.
对自己爸妈，	To their own parents,
要尽力服侍孝敬到底。	They should give full care and respect.
像小鸡出壳你一生下地，	Like chickens out of the shell,
呱呱哭着乱滚乱动。	You were born kicking and crying.
阿爸怕你冷了，	Afraid that you might catch cold,

汪咀达玛
Wangzuidama

吃着的烟筒丢一边，	Papa put aside his smoking pipe,
赶忙拿柴火烧旺火塘；	And hurried to add fuel to the fireplace;
阿妈怕你冷了，	Worried that you might catch cold,
软软的棉花包了一层又一层，	Mama wrapped you with layers of cotton,
紧紧抱在怀里让你暖和。	And held you tightly in her arms to keep you warm.
亲亲的阿爸阿妈，	Your dear Papa and Mama
时时把你放在心窝里。	Always put you in their hearts.
阿爸抱着你喝酒，	Papa drank wine holding you,
香香的酒甜到心窝，	Feeling sweet in his heart.
你要撒尿了，	You were about to pee,
阿爸赶忙放下筷子，	So Papa hastened to put down his chopsticks,
轻轻撑开你的脚。	And stretched your legs gently.
黄黄的尿撒在地上，	Yellow urine sprinkled on the ground,
臭气冲进阿爸的喉咙，	And the stench rushed into Papa's throat.
亲亲的阿爸不发火，	Dear Papa never lost his temper,
等你撒完尿照样把酒喝。	But just resumed his drinking after you were done.
阿妈抱着你吃饭，	Mama had dinner holding you,
香香的米饭甜在心窝，	Feeling sweet in her heart.
你要撒屎了，	You were about to poop,
阿妈赶忙搁下饭碗，	So Mama put down her bowl hastily,
轻轻撑开你的小腿脚。	And stretched your legs gently.
黄稀稀的屎沾衣襟，	When her clothes got stained,

十二奴局 // Twelve Nujus

亲亲的阿妈不动气,	Dear Mama was not angry,
等把你料理干净,	But cleaned up all your mess,
才顾得上把饭碗端起。	Then continued to eat.

你人嫩鼻孔细,　　　　　　　When your tender nostrils
浓浓的鼻涕阻塞换气,　　　　Got plugged with mucus,
张口咽不下奶水,　　　　　　You had trouble swallowing your milk,
换气响得像口熬稀饭的土锅。　Breathing like a pot boiling congee.
阿爸和阿妈,　　　　　　　　Your Papa and Mama,
怕把你嫩嫩的鼻子擤烂,　　　To save your tender nose from hurt,
用嘴含着你的小鼻子,　　　　Put their mouths to your little nose,
一口一口把鼻涕吸出。　　　　And sucked out the mucus.

你人小还不懂事,　　　　　　You were too young to know better,
见着什么就要什么,　　　　　And asked for whatever you saw.
见树上的核桃,　　　　　　　Seeing the walnuts on the tree,
指着要一个,　　　　　　　　You asked for one,
可是树上的核桃,　　　　　　But the walnuts on the tree
青青果皮还没有裂壳。　　　　Still had their green peels on.

阿妈为使你欢喜,　　　　　　Your Mama, to make you happy,
连忙支起小土锅,　　　　　　Promptly put out a small pot,
煮个大鸡蛋,　　　　　　　　And boiled an egg
染上绿色让你吃着。　　　　　In green dye for you to eat.

汪咀达玛
Wangzuidama

你见别人吃多衣果，	Seeing others eating duoyi①,
嚷着也要吃果果。	You cried out for it.
你吃一半丢一半，	You tossed away half of your fruit,
伸着小手要一个又一个。	And kept reaching out for new ones.
阿妈为了满足你，	Your Mama, to pick up duoyi for you,
一天上树摘三次多衣果。	Climbed up the trees three times a day.
你见着天上的星星，	Seeing the stars in the sky,
嚷着要一颗，	You cried out for one.
阿爸没法摘给你，	It was beyond your Papa's reach,
你的眼泪淌成一条小河。	And your tears were streaming.
为了不使你失望，	To save you from despair,
阿爸捉来萤火虫逗你快活。	Papa caught fireflies to cheer you up.
你见着天上的月亮，	Seeing the moon in the sky,
嚷着要一个，	You cried out for one.
阿妈没法拿给你，	As it was beyond your mama's reach,
你差点把阿妈的脸撕破。	You almost left a mark scratching her face.
为了不让你伤心，	To make you feel better,
阿妈伤透了脑筋，	Mama racked her brains.
踩一块雪白的糯米粑粑，	She made a white glutinous rice cake,
给你抱着尽情玩乐。	For you to play with to your heart's content.

① A kind of wild fruit. —Translator's note

十二奴局 // Twelve Nujus

你长大了一点，	As you grew older,
像只跳上跳下的松鼠。	You were like a jumping squirrel.
热和和的春天，	In the warm spring,
你拖着锄头当马骑，	You pretended the hoe was a horse,
嘿哧嘿哧骑到门前，	And with great effort rode it to the door,
又拖着往寨子边走去。	Then dragged it out of the village.
骑马的游戏玩够了，	When you were done with the riding game,
你把锄头丢在草坪上。	You left the hoe on the lawn.
阿爸和阿妈，	Your Papa and Mama,
要去挖田种地，	About to do farm work,
找不见锄头，	But unable to find their hoe,
急得像热锅上的蚂蚁。	Were restless like ants on a hot pot.
阿妈气得流眼泪，	Mama wept in anxiety,
阿爸只好低头向人家借。	And Papa swallowed his pride to go borrowing.
火一样热的夏天，	In the fiery summer,
乌云一来就下雨。	Dark clouds suggested a coming rain.
像小鸭子见到水塘，	Like a duckling at the sight of a pond,
你听到水响就欢喜。	You were happy to hear the rain.
悄悄跑出家门口，	Quietly you ran out of the door,
不卷裤脚就跳下泥塘里，	And jumped in the mud without rolling up your pants.
开一条沟引水，	You dug a trench to channel the water,

汪咀达玛
Wangzuidama

打道埂堵做田学使犁。	And pretended to plow the field you opened.
玩饱玩够出水来，	When you were out of it contented,
新新的衣裳沾满烂泥，	Your new clothes were covered with mud.
阿爸一天给你洗三次澡，	Three times a day Papa bathed you;
阿妈一天给你换三回衣。	Three times a day Mama changed your clothes.

瓜果熟了的秋天，	In the fruitful autumn,
你成了一只树上的猴子。	You became a monkey on a tree.
只要枝头还有梨果，	Fruit on the branches
一天不知爬树多少次。	Were the reason you climbed the trees time and again.
新新的衣裳撕得开花，	New clothes were torn to pieces,
厚厚的裤子磨出口子。	While holes were found in thick pants.
阿爸一天要到树下叫你三回，	Three times a day Papa went to the tree to get you home;
阿妈一天要给你补衣裳三次。	Three times a day Mama mended your clothes.

牛马不出厩的冬天，	In winter when animals stayed in the stable,
茫茫寒雾从四方升起。	The village was clouded in cold misty air.
家里的火塘还未冒烟，	When the fire was yet to be lit,
你就偷着上山撵雀逗趣。	You sneaked out to the hill to catch birds.
太阳都落山了，	By the time of sunset,
饭凉三回又热三回，	Three times the cold meal had been heated,
不见你的影子在哪里。	But there was still no trace of you.
阿妈焦得到森林边呼唤，	Worried, Mama went to the forest calling you;
阿爸急得四处寻找你的足迹。	Anxious, Papa looked for you everywhere.

十二奴局 // Twelve Nujus

过年过节的时候，	When the new year came,
你嚷着要穿新衣。	You cried out for new clothes.
家里没有银子钱，	To get the money,
阿爸阿妈生方打主意：	Your parents did whatever they could:
天不亮阿妈上山背柴卖，	Before dawn Mama went gathering wood to sell,
太阳落山阿爸还在外卖苦力，	While after sunset Papa was still laboring outside.
一滴血汗一分钱，	Every penny was earned by hard toil.
你能穿上新衣裳不容易。	It was not easy to dress you with new clothes.

五荒六月闹饥荒，	May and June saw the great famine,
家里找不出一粒米，	And not a single grain of rice could be found,
阿妈愁得泪汪汪，	Which worried Mama to tears
阿爸焦得满脸成了老树皮。	And wrinkled Papa's face to old bark.
阿爸阿妈为不让你饿坏，	To save you from hunger,
走遍寨头寨脚把米借。	They crossed the whole village to borrow rice.
一丝细雨落干田，	Just like a light drizzle falling on the dry field,
借来一碗米难以充饥。	A bowl of rice can hardly keep off hunger.

为了养活你，	In order to feed you,
阿爸上山挖野菜，	Papa went digging wild herbs uphill,
进森林被猛兽毒蛇吓得魂飞，	And was scared dumb by the vipers and beasts;
钻草窠给倒钩刺划破背脊。	His back got barbed crossing the bushes.
挖一背野菜，	A basket of wild herbs

汪咀达玛
Wangzuidama

流的血汗如下一场雨。	Were earned with a rain of sweat and blood.
阿妈低头出家门，	Mama swallowed her pride,
挨村串寨去讨借。	Begging for food from door to door.
来到寨头被恶狗咬，	She had been attacked by fierce dogs;
下到寨脚受恶人欺。	And bullied by the villains in the village.
伸手讨饭抖碎了心，	It broke her heart to beg;
讨一碗饭流一脸泪。	A bowl of rice came with bitter tears.
阿爸挖来了野菜，	Papa brought wild herbs,
阿妈讨来了饭和米，	And Mama carried home rice.
野菜阿爸阿妈咽，	Herbs were for your parents,
米饭一颗一粒留给你。	While the precious rice was for you.
阿妈饿成了扁豆，	In hunger Mama shrunk like a lentil,
阿爸瘦得像条干鱼。	And papa wizened like a dry fish.
艰难困苦的日子，	Hard times
像数不尽的树叶。	Were like countless leaves.
能换的东西换完了，	Whatever could be pawned had been pawned,
能卖的东西已卖出去，	Whatever could be sold had been sold,
阿爸和阿妈，	Papa and Mama
唯独没有舍得卖你。	Still could not bear to sell you.
省吃俭用积谷米，	They pinched and scraped on the grain,
为的是饥荒年成有饭吃。	To prepare for the famine year.
阿爸阿妈尽心养育你，	Papa and mama did their best raising you,

十二奴局 // Twelve Nujus

盼你像春笋一样快长，	Hoping you would grow fast as spring shoots,
一节一节长成树。	Into a full-grown tree.
阿妈的心血操干了，	Mama has exhausted her energy,
阿爸的力气使尽了，	And Papa his strength.
你已长成大人，	Now you have become an adult,
讨了媳妇当家立业。	Starting your own family.
像转磨一样轮到你了，	Now the mill is turned to your hands,
切莫把阿爸阿妈的恩情忘记。	Don't forget to repay their kindness.
阿妈的脸上垒起沟埂，	Mama's face now has lines,
阿爸的头上落上了一层银霜。	And Papa's hair is grizzled.
世上的人哟，	People of this world,
个个都要老一回，	All will grow old someday.
做儿女的人哟，	Being sons and daughters,
不要学山雀硬了翅膀不回窝，	You should never copy the ungrateful tits,
要拿出一片诚心来孝敬老人，	But look after your parents with your whole heart,
让他们日子过得快活。	And help them live happily.
为了养育你，	In order to raise you,
阿爸阿妈挣伤了腰杆，	Your parents have worn out their spines,
苦损了筋骨。	And tired their bones.
无论生活有多艰难，	No matter how hard life is,
无论活计有多繁忙，	How busy you are,
切莫叫阿爸阿妈出家门，	You should never call your parents out of the door,

汪咀达玛
Wangzuidama

上山下地干活计。	To labor in the hills or fields.

磨损的刀难砍柴， Just as worn knives are hard to cut wood with,
上了年纪的人牙脱落。 Aged people see their teeth off.
阿爸阿妈吃的要精心做： Be particular about what they eat:
饭要煮得泡软， Rice is to be cooked soft,
菜要切细煮烂， And vegetables tender,
让他们吃得又香又甜。 So that they can fully enjoy the meal.

家里办事情， Any family matter
先要和阿爸阿妈商量； Is to be discussed with them;
家里有好吃的东西， Anything delicious
先要给阿爸阿妈尝； Is to be tasted first by them;
过年过节杀鸡鸭， When chickens and ducks are killed on big days,
嫩肉和肝要给阿爸阿妈送上。 Tender meat and liver are for them.
阿爸喜欢喝口酒， Papa likes drinking wine,
家里的酒壶不要空； So never let the jug be empty.
母亲喜欢烧火塘取暖， Mama likes warming herself by the fire,
灶前的柴堆不要空。 So make sure the firewood is always in supply.

阿爸阿妈老来脚手硬， As their limbs turn stiff,
出出进进不灵便。 It is hard for them to move about.
不论到寨子里串门子， Whether they drop in on their neighbors',
或是走亲串戚到他乡； Or visit relatives in the distance;

十二奴局 // Twelve Nujus

不论出门去做客，	Whether they were invited,
或是去看望朋友，	Or called on by their friends,
做儿女的要多加留意，	You should keep an eye on them,
送去接回尽儿女心肠。	Help them with their travel thoughtfully.

阿爸阿妈老来怕风寒，
防寒保暖记在心上。
要趁天气还不冷，
早早缝好过冬的衣裳。
十冬腊月到山寨，
不让阿爸阿妈受寒冻，
儿女要多砍些柴，
白天黑夜把火塘烧旺。

The elders are vulnerable to cold,
So often remind them of keeping warm.
Before it is cold,
Prepare them winter clothes.
In the dead of winter,
To keep them from the freezing cold,
You should collect more firewood
To keep the fire burning through the days and nights.

世间的儿女，
这是孝敬爸妈的道理；
道理是人间的种子，
一天也不能让它打失；
一代一代传下去，
世世代代兴下去。
众：萨—萨！

All children of the world,
This is the way we honor our parents.
Like a precious seed,
This truth should never be lost;
Let it known to all our offspring,
From generation to generation.
Chorus: Sah-Sah!

觉车里祖
Jueche Lizu*

---

* 觉车里祖：即觉车赶街。
　Jueche Lizu means the fairs started by Jueche.

十二奴局 // Twelve Nujus

萨啦阿依——
最先建街子的是哪个？
最先赶街子的是哪个？
最先建街子的是觉车，
最先赶街子的是汉人。
最先建起来的街子是哪个？
最热闹的街子是哪个？
最先建起来的是烘阿欧德额里①街，
最热闹的是汉人地方的斗楚②街。

觉麻三弟兄建起麻密寨，
觉麻在麻密寨安了家。
不赶街子不痛快，
不赶街子不热闹。

觉车离开麻密寨，
到各个地方赶街子。
最先建起来的街子是哪个？

① 欧德额里：古地名。
② 斗楚：古地名。

Sala Ayi–
Who was the first to build a market?
Who was the first to hold fairs?
Jueche was the first to build a market;
The Han were the first to hold fairs.
Which was the first market ever built?
Where was the most lively fair held?
The Oude'eli① market in Hong'a was the first ever built,
And the most lively fair was held in the Han Douchu② street.

After building the Mami Village with his brothers,
Juema settled down there.
Without a market he felt unhappy,
Without fairs he felt lonely.

Jueche then left the Mami Village,
In search of a market place.
Which was the first market ever built?

① An ancient place.
② An ancient place.

觉车里祖
Jueche Lizu

最热闹的街子是哪个？	Where was the most lively fair held?
最先建起来的是烘阿欧德额里街，	The Oude'eli market in Hong'a was the first ever built,
最热闹的是汉人地方的斗楚街。	And the most lively fair was held in the Han Douchu street.
觉车来到了窀特①地方，	He arrived at the place of Zhunte①,
转来转去眼睛四处瞧。	Looking around to see:
高高的山底下，	Just below the mountain,
清清的龙潭旁，	Beside the clear wellspring,
密密的树林中间，	Amidst the dense woods,
有一块宽宽的平地，	There was a land wide and flat,
是个赶街的好地方。	Which looked perfect for a market place.
觉车跑到各个村寨，	Jueche ran to the villages,
把赶街的事情告诉人们：	Informing the people of a fair:
"龙日是个吉祥的日子，	"On the auspicious Day of the Dragon,
窀特地方要赶龙街。	A Dragon Fair will be held in Zhunte.
街上买吃的人老实多，	The fair will be full of people buying food,
要卖吃的就去赶龙街；	So be there if you have any to sell;
街上买穿的人老实多，	The fair will be full of people buying clothes,
要卖穿的就去赶龙街；	So be there if you have any to sell;
街上买用的东西老实多，	The fair will be full of people buying appliances,
要卖用的东西就去赶龙街。	So be there if you have any to sell.
街上吃的东西样样有，	Various kinds of food will be there for trade,

---

① 窀特：即浪堤，在今红河县境。　① It is in today's Honghe County.

十二奴局 // Twelve Nujus

要换吃的就去龙街上；	So be there if you are in need;
街上穿的东西样样有，	Various kinds of clothes will be there for trade,
要换穿的就去龙街上；	So be there if you are in need;
街上用的东西样样有，	Various kinds of appliances will be there for trade,
要换用的就去龙街上。"	So be there if you are in need."

到了属龙那一天，	On the Day of the Dragon,
赶街的人像沟水一样淌来。	People flooded to the fair.
赶马做生意的汉人来了，	Han men came with carts of goods;
穿宽袖衣裳的傣家妇女来了，	Dai women came in wide-sleeved clothes;
穿短裤的叶车姑娘来了，	Yeche girls came wearing short pants;
戴公鸡帽的彝家姑娘来了，	Yi girls came wearing rooster-shaped hats;
会打麂子的仆拉汉子来了，	Pula men, known as muntjac-hunters, came;
穿短衣裳的罗美老表来了，	Luomei people came wearing shorts.
各种各样的人都来了，	All walks of life had come,
四面八方的人都来了。	From far and wide.

龙街街子老实热闹，	The fair became so crowded,
赶街的人像蚂蚁一样多。	With people swarming like ants.
赶街人的声音，	People visiting the fair
像打雷一样响。	Sounded as loud as thunder.
街上吃的东西样样有：	The fair was full of all kinds of food:
通海的黄烟黄生生，	Yellow cigarettes from Tonghai,
石屏的白鱼亮晶晶，	Shiny white fish from Shiping,

觉车里祖
Jueche Lizu

汉人的冰糖甜又脆，	Sweet and crisp sugar brought by the Han,
仆拉的茄子有碓嘴粗，	Pestle-like eggplants by the Pula,
哈尼的泥鳅黄鳝老实肥，	Fat loaches and mud eels by the Hani,
卷粉凉粉到处摆，	Noodles and bean jelly were seen everywhere,
猪肉牛肉满街香……	While the whole street smelled of pork and beef...
街上穿的东西样样有：	The fair was full of things to wear:
汉人的丝线刺眼睛，	Dazzling silk thread brought by the Han,
白布花布俏生生，	As well as fabrics of different colors;
彝家的棉花白花花，	Snow white cotton brought by the Yi,
银子镯头亮闪闪，	Together with silver bracelets;
染布的蓝靛青幽幽，	Indigo blue dyes were for sale;
鞋子帽子摆成一排排，	Row after row were shoes and hats,
衣裳裤子摆成一层层。	Layer upon layer were shirts and pants.
街上用的东西样样有：	The fair was full of tools:
锄头斧子砍刀摆地上，	Hoes, axes and machetes were put on the ground,
犁耙簸箕篾箩放地上；	Along with rakes, dustpans and crates;
叶车人织的席子滑噜噜，	Mats woven by Yeche were smooth,
仆拉人编的背箩铁扎扎；	While back-baskets by Pula were solid;
大小银针一包包，	Bags of silver needles came in all sizes,
麻布口袋一打打，	Gunny sacks in dozens,
土锅瓦罐堆一片。	While pots and crocks were in piles.

十二奴局 // Twelve Nujus

街子边边上，	At the corner of the market,
卖的大猪小猪一窝窝，	For sale were litters of pigs and piglets;
黄牛水牛骡马一大场，	Herds of buffalo, cattle and mules,
鸡鸭装在笼子里，	Chickens and ducks in coops,
狗像牛角弯弯地躺在地上，	Dogs lying on the floor like ox horns,
山羊哞哞叫，	Bleating goats,
小猫在鸡笼里抓。	And kittens kept in cages.
要买的东西买着啰，	People bought whatever they wanted,
要卖的东西卖掉啰；	And sold whatever they wanted;
小伙子瞧着姑娘啰，	Young men fell in love with girls,
小姑娘遇着伙子啰。	While girls met with young men.
赶街大家都好玩，	Everybody had fun at the fair;
赶街大家都喜欢。	Everybody liked it very much.
从此一到属龙的日子，	Since then every Day of the Dragon,
大家都来赶街啰。	All would come to visit the fair.
觉车高兴了，	Jueche was happy;
觉车欢喜了，	Jueche was full of joy.
单赶一个街子太孤单，	But a single fair was not enough,
还要建更多的街子才热闹。	It took more to liven things up.
觉车又转到别处，	Jueche then turned elsewhere,
去选赶街的地方。	Looking for places to hold fairs.

觉车里祖
Jueche Lizu

觉车来到叶车地方，	Jueche then arrived at Yeche,
转来转去到处瞧，	Looking around to see:
看见高高的山底下，	At the foot of the tall mountain,
宽宽的坎子旁边，	Beside the broad field,
长长的河上面，	Upstream of the long river,
一个大大的垭口上，	On the wide gap between two hills,
有一块宽宽的草坪，	There was a wide lawn,
是个赶街的好地方。	Which looked perfect as a market place.
觉车跑到各个寨子，	Jueche ran to each village,
把赶街的事情告诉人们：	Informing people of a fair:
"羊日是个吉祥的日子，	"On the auspicious Day of the Sheep,
叶车地方要赶羊街① 啰。	A Sheep Fair① will be held in Yeche.
街上的东西老实多，	The fair will be full of goods,
要买东西就去赶羊街；	So be there if you want to buy anything;
街上买东西的人老实多，	The fair will be full of buyers,
要卖东西的就去赶羊街。	So be there if you have anything to sell;
街上俏俏的姑娘老实多，	The fair will be full of pretty girls,
要瞧姑娘的就去赶羊街；	So be there if you want to meet girls;
街上称称② 的伙子老实多，	The fair will be full of handsome young men,
要瞧伙子的就去赶羊街。"	So be there if you want to meet them."

---

① 羊街：在红河县境内。
② 称称：标致、漂亮的意思。

① A place in oday's Honghe County.

十二奴局 // Twelve Nujus

到了属羊那一天，	On the Day of the Sheep,
赶街的人像搬家的蚂蚁一样走来。	People swarmed the fair like moving ants.
背戥子做生意的汉人来了，	Han men came with portable scales on their backs;
挑竹篮的傣家伙子来了，	Dai men came carrying bamboo baskets;
会打马鹿的瑶家来了，	Yao people, good at deer hunting, came;
戴白布帽的叶车女人来了，	Yeche women came wearing white hats;
戴银泡帽的彝家姑娘来了，	Yi girls came wearing silver-decorated hats;
穿短衣裳的罗美人来了。	Luomei people came wearing shorts.
各种各样的人都来了，	All walks of life had come,
四面八方的人都来了。	From far and wide.

羊街街子老实热闹，	The Sheep Fair became very crowded,
赶街的人有一升芝麻多，	With people like countless sesames.
街场上的说话声，	They produced a loud sound,
像雨天暴发的洪水一样响。	Like floods on rainy days.
街上吃的东西样样有：	The fair was full of all kinds of food:
玉溪的烟丝黄生生，	Yellow tobacco from Yuxi,
新平的酒药白花花，	White yeast from Xinping;
磨黑的盐巴一驮驮，	Packs of salt from Mohei,
元江的红糖一箩箩，	Baskets of brown sugar from Yuanjiang,
傣家的荔枝甜蜜蜜，	Sweet lychees brought by the Dai,
彝家的花生香噜噜，	Tasty peanuts by the Yi,
哈尼的螺蛳一背背，	Baskets of spiral shells by the Hani,

觉车里祖
Jueche Lizu

仆拉的粗烟一把把，	Bundles of tobacco leaves by the Pula,
叶车的谷子黄灿灿，	Yellow millet brought by the Yeche,
罗美的大米齐刷刷，	Even-grained rice by the Luomei,
米线卷粉到处摆，	Rice noodles were seen everywhere,
猪肉牛肉炒得满街香。	While the whole street smelled of pork and beef.

街上穿的戴的样样有： The fair was full of all kinds of things to wear:
白布青布滑噜噜， White and blue fabrics felt smooth,
银链银镯亮闪闪， While silver necklaces and bracelets looked shiny,
丝线花辫惹人爱， And braided silk threads appeared to be so adorable;
衣裳裤子摆得一层层， Layer upon layer were shirts and pants;
鞋子帽子摆得一排排。 Row after row were shoes and hats.

街上用的东西样样有： The fair was full of tools:
锄头镰刀摆地上， Hoes and sickles on the ground,
谷船筶桌置地上， Along with boat-shaped containers and bamboo tables;
叶车的蓑衣大又厚， Thick and wide coir raincoats brought by the Yeche;
临安的瓦货排成行， Tiles from Lin'an stacked in rows;
通海的小刀快又亮， Shiny and sharp knives from Tonghai.
街子边的草地上， On the lawn by the market,
一大场黄牛躺在树荫下， A large herd of cattle lay in the shade of the trees.
拴在桩桩上的大猪小猪摇尾巴， Pigs and piglets, tied to piles, wagged their tails.
鸡鸭一笼笼， Chickens and ducks were in coops,
红脚杆鸽子一对对， While red-legged doves were in pairs,

十二奴局 // Twelve Nujus

拴着的狗哭叫着咬索子。	And dogs on leash barked while biting ropes.

需要的东西买着啰, People bought whatever they wanted,
背来的东西卖掉啰; And sold everything they brought;
小伙子看上了心爱的姑娘啰, Young men met girls they loved,
姑娘跟合心的伙子订好约会啰。 And girls dated guys they liked.
赶街人人都得到好处, All reaped benefits from the fair;
赶街人人都得到欢乐, All gained happiness from the fair.
从此一到属羊的日子, Since then every Day of the Sheep,
大家都来赶羊街。 Everyone came to visit the Sheep Fair.

觉车高兴了, Jueche was happy;
觉车欢喜了, Jueche was full of joy.
可是他还不满足, But he was not satisfied,
还要赶更多的街子。 He wanted more fairs.

觉车转到各个地方, He explored many new places,
去建新新的街子: Setting up new fairs:
转到车乌① 赶牛街, Cattle Fairs were to be held in Chewu①,
转到打勐② 赶猪街, Pig Fairs in Dameng②,
转到阿丕③ 赶马街, Horse Fairs in Api③,

---

① 在红河县境内。　　① In Honghe County.
② 在元江县境内。　　② In Yuanjiang County.
③ 在红河县境内。　　③ In Honghe County.

觉车里祖
Jueche Lizu

转到保玛① 赶鼠街，	Rat Fairs in Baoma①,
转到西笎② 赶兔街，	Rabbit Fairs in Xizhun②,
转到河坝赶虎街③。	Tiger Fairs in Heba③.
他转遍了各个地方，	He had traveled far and wide,
十二个日子都赶起街了。	Assigning twelve fairs to twelve days.

觉车高兴了，	Jueche was happy;
觉车欢喜了，	Jueche was full of joy.
可是单赶十二个日子的街不如意，	But twelve days of fairs were not enough,
还要赶更多的街子。	He wanted more fairs.

觉车来到瓦渣④ 地方，	Jueche then arrived at Wazha④,
转来转去到处瞧：	Looking around to see:
看见高高的山脚下，	At the foot of the high mountain,
宽宽的坝子上边，	Over the broad basin,
清清的龙潭旁，	Beside the clear wellspring,
有一块宽宽的草坪，	There was a wide lawn,
是个赶街的好地方。	Which looked perfect for a market place.
觉车跑到各个寨子，	Jueche ran to each village
把赶街的事情告诉人们：	Informing people of a fair:

---

① 在红河县境内。 ① In Honghe County.
② 在元江县境内。 ② In Yuanjiang County.
③ 在红河县境内。 ③ In Honghe County.
④ 在元江县境内。 ④ In Yuanjiang County.

十二奴局 // Twelve Nujus

"老博①是个好地方，
大家快去赶老博街了。

街上样样东西都有，
要买哪样东西就去赶老博街；
街上好多人等着买东西，
要卖哪样东西就去赶老博街；
街上的姑娘像花一样俏，
要瞧姑娘就去赶老博街；
街上的伙子像金竹一样标直，
要找男人就去赶老博街。"

到了赶街那一天，
赶街的人像回窝的蜜蜂一样飞来。
赶马做生意的汉人来了，
挑竹篮的傣家来了，
戴包头的哈尼姑娘来了，
抬烟锅的彝家伙子来了，
敢打老虎的瑶家汉子来了，
会喝酒的仆拉老倌来了。
各种各样的人都来了，
四面八方的人都来了。

① 在红河县境内。

"Laobo① is a good place,
A fair will be held there.

Everything is there for sale,
So be there if you need anything;
There are a lot of people waiting to buy things,
So be there if you want to sell anything.
Girls there are as pretty as flowers,
So be there if you want to meet girls;
Young men there are as handsome as bamboo trees,
So be there to get yourself a man."

On the Fair Day,
People flocked to the market like bees returning to hives.
Han men came with carts of goods;
Dai people came carrying bamboo baskets;
Hani girls came wearing folded hats;
Yi guys came carrying smoking pots;
Yao men, known as tiger hunters, came;
Old Pula drinkers came.
All walks of life had come,
From far and wide.

① In Honghe County.

觉车里祖
Jueche Lizu

老博街子老实热闹，	The Laobo Fair was very crowded,
赶街人像山上的树一样多，	With people as numerous as trees in the hills.
街场的喧哗声，	The hustling and bustling of the fair
像野火烧山一样响。	Sounded like a mountain in a wild fire.

街上吃的东西样样有：　　　　The fair was full of all kinds of food:
蒙自的刀烟黄生生，　　　　　Yellow tobaccos from Mengzi,
磨黑的盐巴白花花，　　　　　White salt from Mohei,
石屏的白鱼亮闪闪，　　　　　Shiny white fish from Shiping,
建水的红糖红生生，　　　　　Brown sugar from Jianshui,
傣家的杧莓①老实甜，　　　　Sweet mangos brought by the Dai,
伯纳②的荞粑粑香喷喷，　　　Delicious buckwheat cakes from Bona①,
草包鸡蛋鸭蛋一背背，　　　　Bags of eggs wrapped in grass,
淌油的火雀一串串，　　　　　Oil-dripping fried sparrows in strings,
木耳香菌一箩箩，　　　　　　Fungus and mushrooms in full baskets,
刺竹笋子一堆堆。　　　　　　Thorny bamboo shoots in piles,
哈尼的谷子满街场，　　　　　Millet in large amount by the Hani,
彝家的紫米紫又亮；　　　　　Shiny purple rice by the Yi,
卷粉凉粉到处摆，　　　　　　Noodles and bean jelly were seen everywhere,
猪肉牛肉满街香。　　　　　　While the whole market smelled of pork and beef.

街上穿的戴的样样有：　　　　The fair was full of various things to wear:

---

① 杧莓：即杧果。
② 伯纳：在红河县境内。

---

① In Honghe County.

十二奴局 // Twelve Nujus

白布青布滑噜噜，	White and blue fabrics felt smooth,
银链银镯亮闪闪，	While silver necklaces and bracelets looked shiny;
丝线花瓣有七样色，	Braided silk threads came in seven colors,
毛巾花布有七十二种花，	Towels and fabrics with seventy-two patterns;
衣裳裤子摆得一层层，	Layer upon layer were shirts and pants;
鞋子帽子摆得一排排。	Row after row were shoes and hats.
街上用的东西样样有：	The fair was full of tools:
锄头镰刀一把把，	Hoes and sickles in bunches,
背箩饭兜一堆堆，	Back baskets and rice bags in piles,
土锅土缸摆地上，	Pots and crocks on the ground
碗罐瓦盆随人拣，	Along with bowls and basins,
倮卜①的篾帽亮闪闪，	Shiny bamboo hats from Luobo[①],
左能②的席子滑又亮。	Smooth mats from Zuoneng[②].
街子边上哟，	At the corner of the fair,
卖的牛马一群群，	For sale were herds of cattle and horses,
山羊咩咩一帮帮，	Along with bleating goats,
大猪小猪一大片，	Droves of pigs and piglets,
鸡笼鸭笼摆了一大场，	Coops of chickens and ducks,
猫在鸡笼里打瞌睡，	Cats dozing off in the coop,
狗像牛角弯弯地睡在地上。	Dogs sleeping on the floor like horns.

---

① 在红河县境内。
② 在红河县境内。

① In Honghe County.
② In Honghe County.

觉车里祖
Jueche Lizu

要买的东西买着啰，	People bought whatever they wanted,
要卖的东西卖掉啰；	And sold whatever they wanted;
小伙子瞧上姑娘啰，	Young men fell in love with girls,
姑娘瞧着伙子啰。	And girls with young men.
赶街个个都好玩，	All had fun at the fair;
赶街人人都喜欢，	All liked the fair very much.
从此一着老博街，	Since then every Luobo Fair,
大家都从四面八方聚拢来。	People gathered from far and wide.
觉车欢喜啰，	Jueche was full of joy;
觉车高兴了。	Jueche was happy.
可是他还不满足，	But he was not satisfied,
还要赶更多的街子。	He wanted more fairs.
觉车转到各个地方，	He explored many new places,
去建新新的街子。	Setting up new fairs.
转到腊哈①地方赶新街，	New Fair in Laha①,
转到多仰地方赶牛洪街②，	The Niuhong Fair in Duoyang②,
转到伯纳地方赶达德街，	The Dade Fair in Bona,
转到洛恐赶戈比街。	The Gebi Fair in Luokong,
转到思陀赶仰书德街，	The Shude Fair in Situo,
转到老密赶尼保街。	The Niluo Fair in Laomi.

---

① 在红河县境内。
② 多仰、牛洪：在绿春县境内。

① In Honghe County.
② Niuhong and Duoyang in Lüchun County.

十二奴局 // Twelve Nujus

虚洛街子赶起来了，	Then the Xuluo Fair was set up,
里沙街子赶起来了，	And the Lisha Fair,
合然街子赶起来了，	The Heran Fair,
布洪街子赶起来了，	The Buhong Fair,
勐只街子赶起来了，	The Mengzhi Fair,
依玛街子赶起来了……①	The Yima Fair...①

觉车转遍了各个地方，
在世间建起了七十二个街子，
七十二个街子七十二个名字，
各个街子赶起来，
世间一天天热闹起来了。
男女老少都好玩，
四面八方的人都喜欢，
街子一天也不会打失，
人们一天也不会把觉车忘记。
众：萨—萨！

Jueche had traveled far and wide,
Setting up seventy-two fairs,
Each with its own name.
As the fairs were started,
The world was livened up day by day.
Men, women and children all had fun;
People from far and wide liked it.
The fairs would last forever,
For which people will always keep Jueche in mind.
Chorus: Sah-Sah!

---

① 达德、洛恐、戈比、思陀、老密、虚洛、里沙、合然、布洪、勐只、依玛在红河县境内。

① Dade, Luokong, Gebi, Situo, Laomi, Xuluo, Lisha, Heran, Buhong, Mengzhi and Yima in Honghe County.

伙及拉及
Huojilaji*

---

* 伙及拉及：哈尼语，即一年四季。
　Huojilaji means the four seasons of the year in the Hani language.

十二奴局 // Twelve Nujus

冬　月　　　　　　　The Eleventh Month[1]

萨啦阿依——	Sala Ayi–
旧的一年过去，	The old year has gone by,
新的一年[1]开始了。	And the new one comes.[2]
冬月哪样虫虫叫？	What are the insects chirping this month?
草窠里的蛐蛐叫。	Crickets are chirping in the grass.
河坝的雾气，	The fog, rising from the river dam,
像长翅膀一样飞来了；	Flies as if with wings;
冷风刮进寨子，	Cold wind blows into the village,
翻动房头上的茅草；	Flipping the thatch on roofs.
小鸟缩在墙角不动，	Birdies huddled in the corner motionless,
树上的落叶满地跑。	And falling leaves are dancing around.
冬天不来，	If not for the winter,
牛马不得养身子；	Cattle and horses can never rest;
冬天不来，	If not for the winter,
草木不得睡觉。	Plants can never go to sleep;
勤劳的人，	Industrious men,

---

[1] 按哈尼族历法，冬月为一年的岁首。

[1] The months in this book refer to lunar months. –Tnanslator's note
[2] Hani calendar takes the eleventh month as the beginning of a new year.

伙及拉及
Huojilaji

冬天是备耕的好时节，	Winter is a good season for farming preparation.
不要怕冷风像针戳，	Fear not the piercingly cold wind;
不要怕冰水裂开手脚，	Fear not the cracking icy water.
上山砍荞地，	Just go loosen the buckwheat fields uphill,
下山开梯田，	And cultivate terraces downhill.
挖田打埂要抓紧，	Spare no time maintaining the field,
灌满田水心安闲。	And enjoy the leisure only when the paddies are filled.
众：萨—萨！	Chorus: Sah-Sah!

腊　月

The Twelfth Month

萨啦阿依——
旧的一月过去了，
新的一月来到。
高山铺冰雪，
寒雾罩寨子；
大树砍得断，
雾帐撕不开；
地上蛇不跑，
天上虫不飞。
虫为何不飞？
钻进土里去了；
蛇为何不跑？
缩在洞里睡觉。

Sala Ayi–
The old month has gone by,
And the new month comes.
When mountains are covered in snow,
Villages are clouded in chilly mists;
Swords sharp enough to cut trees,
Could not rip open the thick misty air;
No snake is seen crawling on the ground,
And no bug is seen flying in the sky.
Why is no bug flying?
They all worm into the soil.
Why is no snake crawling?
They all curl up in the caves sleeping.

十二奴局 // Twelve Nujus

什么树叶枯树不死？	What trees remain alive with dead leaves?
山坡上的麻栗树。	The chestnut trees on the hillside.
什么树死叶不枯？	What trees die with green leaves on?
山谷里的蕨蕨草。	Ferns in the remote valleys.
高山飘雪花，	When snowflakes fall on the hill,
寨旁的梨树要死一回了，	Pear trees by the village are about to die,
路边的蒿枝要死一回了，	So is the wormwood by the road,
地上的茅草要死一回了。	And grass on the ground.

草枯根不死，
蛆虫冬睡人不要贪闲，
快离开火塘，
把蓑衣披上，
修好田间的水沟，
积满寨边的粪塘。
众：萨—萨！

Just as grass withers with roots alive,
We shall stay active in the dormant winter.
Get away from the fireplace,
With straw cloaks on,
To fix the ditch in the field,
And fill the septic tank by the village.
Chorus: Sah-Sah!

正　月 / The First Month

萨啦阿依——
旧的一月过去了，
新的一月来到。
过了一日变一日，

Sala Ayi–
The old month has gone by,
And the new one comes.
Change takes place every day,

伙及拉及
Huojilaji

翻过一月是一样。	So the new month differs from the old one.
雾气慢慢散开，	As fogs slowly clear up,
竹子尖尖吹笛萧①，	Spring flutes on bamboo tips;
大地醒来了，	The earth is waking up;
大地要翻身了。	The earth is rolling over.

小虫从洞里伸出头，　　Bugs head out of the cave,
树木冒起芽苞，　　And trees begin to bud.
四周听见小虫的叫声，　　Insects are heard humming around,
树林里有鸟叫的声音。　　While birds are chirping in the woods.
河坝里先发芽的是什么树？　　Which trees bud first on the river dam?
河坝里先发芽的是杨柳树。　　The willow trees are the first to bud.
高山上先冒头的是什么草？　　Which grass grows first on the high mountains?
高山上先冒头的是蕨蕨草。　　Ferns are the first to grow.

寨边樱桃开花，　　By the village cherry trees are in bloom,
沟边索可玛依②飘香，　　While the ravines are scented with jasmine orange;
山顶妥底玛依③怒放，　　The hilltop flames with azaleas,
河坝攀枝花染红树梢。　　And on the river dam Kapok tree tops are tinted red.
正月来了，　　Here comes the first month,
鸟儿飞出来找食。　　When birds fly out to find food.

---

① 春风吹竹梢发出的响声。
② 哈尼语，即七里香花。
③ 哈尼语，一种红杜鹃花。

十二奴局 // Twelve Nujus

最先飞来的是燕子，	Swallows are the first to arrive,
布谷鸟也跟着飞来了。	Followed by cuckoos.
燕子从哪里飞来？	Where do the swallows come from?
从遥远的沙咪中仰①飞来，	They are from the distant island,
那里有茫茫的格通②，	In the middle of the vast sea,
还有九重高的围墙。	Which is blocked by nine high walls.
布谷从哪里飞来？	Where do the cuckoos come from?
从遥远的沙咪中仰飞来，	They are from the distant island,
那里有茫茫的格通大海，	In the middle of the vast sea,
还有九重高的围墙。	Which is blocked by nine high walls.
格通大海有多宽？	How wide is the sea?
哈南③要飞七天。	It takes ravens seven days to fly across.
格通大海有多长？	How long is the sea?
鸿回④要飞十个早上。	It takes turtledoves ten days to cross.
燕子飞过大海，	Swallows fly over the sea.
布谷飞过大海。	Cuckoos fly over the sea.
燕子先飞到哈沙⑤，	Swallows first reach Yuanjiang,
布谷跟着飞到哈沙。	Followed by cuckoos.
一只飞到傣家河坝，	One flies to the river dams of the Dai,

---

① 哈尼语，即大海中的岛。
② 哈尼语，即大海。
③ 哈尼语，即乌鸦。
④ 哈尼语，即斑鸠。
⑤ 哈尼语，即元江。

伙及拉及
Huojilaji

一只飞到汉人地方，	One to where the Han live,
一只飞到哈尼山乡。	One to the hilly areas of the Hani,
一路飞来一路叫：	Chirping all the way:
春天来到了！	Here comes the spring!
燕子飞进山寨，	Swallows fly into the villages,
燕窝筑在屋梁上，	Building nests on the roof.
燕子九年不搬家，	For nine years they would not move,
旧家上面盖新房。	But just build new nests on top of the old ones.
燕子欢喜地叫，	Cheerfully swallows twitter:
春耕的时间到了；	It's time for spring plowing.
布谷欢喜地叫，	Happily cuckoos chirp:
安排活计的日子来到。	It's time to make plans.
万事万物醒了，	All things wake up;
万事万物动了。	All things are alive.
正月到，	In the first month,
男人爱想女人，	Men think of women,
女人爱想男人；	And women think of men;
家里的禽畜动起来了，	All farm animals become active,
不动的没有了。	With no exception.
大公鸡冠子闪亮，	Roosters with shiny combs
飞上屋顶啼叫，	Jump to the roof crowing,
忙爬粪塘糠堆去了；	Or peck chaff in the dirt;

十二奴局 // Twelve Nujus

鸭子翅膀下水，	Ducks flap into the water,
抬起头嘎嘎叫；	Strutting and quacking;
黄狗蹦上蹦下，	Yellow dogs jump up and down,
使劲在灰地上扒窝；	Digging hard in the dirt;
小公猪东窜西窜，	Young boars scurry here and there,
一步不离跟母猪跑；	Courting sows closely.
公羊晃动长角，	Rams shake their long horns,
追逐母羊吃草；	Chasing ewes and grazing;
马儿扬起鬃毛，	Horses raise their manes,
闪开四蹄撒欢；	Galloping and frisking;
水牛摇动尾巴，	Buffalos wag their tails,
在泥塘里打滚……	Rolling in the mud…
正月到，	In the first month,
山野的鸟兽动起来了：	Birds and beasts in the wild come to life:
松林鹧鸪飞，	Partridges fly in the woods,
草丛鹌鹑叫，	Quail coo in the grass,
山上马鹿跃，	Deer leap in the hills,
山凹草豹叫，	Leopards roar in the valleys,
山沟野猪闹，	Wild boars frolic by the ravines,
崖边麂子跳……	Muntjac hop by the cliffs…
正月到，	In the first month,
水里的鱼虫动起来了：	Fish and water bugs come to life:

伙及拉及
Huojilaji

杂草下泥鳅摆尾，	Loaches swim in the weeds,
浮萍下鱼儿翻起波浪，	Fish stir the water under the duckweed,
泥塘里蚯蚓扭动腰肢，	Earthworms twist their bodies in the mud,
田水中虾巴虫舞蹈。	Shrimps dance in the paddy.

正月到， In the first month,
五谷籽种动起来： Seeds of crops come to life:
簸箩里的谷种伸腰， Millet seeds stretch in the bamboo basket,
豆荚里的豆种眨眼， Bean seeds blink their eyes in the pods;
封火楼上芋头冒芽喷喷响。 Taro sprouts upstairs squeaking.

燕子叫了， Chirping swallows
春耕的时节来到； Suggest the time of spring plowing
布谷鸟叫了， Singing cuckoos
下种的时节来到； Indicate the time of seed sowing.
挖田种地的人， Those who farm for a living
闲着的心痒起来了。 Could not stay idle anymore.
鸡肥要看好鸡种， Good breeds promise fat chickens,
谷壮要靠好谷种。 While good seeds promise high yields.
筛子筛谷种， Seeds are to be sifted,
簸箕簸谷种， And to be winnowed.
秕谷落下地， In this way chaff is removed,
谷种箩里装。 And corn seeds remain in the basket.

十二奴局 // Twelve Nujus

清水泡谷种，	Seeds are then soaked
瓦缸泡谷种，	In clear water in crocks.
鸡蛋献一个，	One egg is to be offered
谷神来保佑。	To the god of grain for his blessing.

小鸡要由母鸡抱，	Chickens are hatched by hens,
谷种要用树叶捂。	While grain seeds are kept warm in leaves.
哪样树叶才暖和？	What leaves keep them warm?
宽厚的泡桐树叶最暖和。	Broad Paulownia tree leaves are the best warmers.
采回泡桐叶，	With leaves collected,
背箩捂谷种。	Grain seeds are put in the baskets.
冷水浇三次，	Which are drenched with water,
热水浇三回，	Cold and hot, each three times.
三天三夜盖被子，	For three days and nights the baskets are covered
根芽出来白生生。	Before the seeds sprout white.

快整好寨脚的秧田，	Get the paddies down the village leveled,
谷种要叫阿爸了，	As the seeds are about to meet their dad,
寨脚平滑的秧田阿爸等它；	The flat paddies down the village;
谷种要叫阿妈了，	In need of milk and a hug,
谷种要吃奶水了，	The seeds are about to call for their mom,
龙潭边的秧田阿妈来抱它。	The paddies beside the wellspring.

背出谷种撒秧田，	The grain seeds are carried to the paddies,

伙及拉及
Huojilaji

上埂撒三把,	Where three handfuls are cast in the upper area,
下埂撒三把,	Three handfuls in the lower area,
中间撒三把。	And three handfuls in the middle area.
撒谷种要雨点样均匀,	They should be spread as evenly as raindrops,
要像姑娘帽子上的银泡花。	Or as the silver flowers on girls' hats.

谷种的奶汁是哪样? — What is the milk for the grain seeds?
龙潭里出来的清泉水。 — The clear water from the wellspring.
看秧田要像照管娃娃, — Look after the paddies as if they were your children,
不要让牛马、鼠雀糟蹋。 — And protect them from the cattle, horses, rats and sparrows.
一天要放三回水, — Three times a day they will be watered;
一天要洒三回水, — Three times a day they will be sprinkled,
让谷种快快成长。 — Which will make sure they grow fast.

谷种撒下去, — After the seeds are planted,
大田要翻犁, — The fields need plowing.
犁耙没有牛, — Without yoked oxen,
脚手粗壮难种田。 — The plow is hard to drive even for strong hands.

请问寨头的长老, — Respected elders in the village were consulted:
犁田的牛去哪里找? — Where to find the plowing oxen?
犁田的牛松格① 这地方有, — They can be bought in the place of Songge①,

---

① 在红河县境内。

① A place in Houghe County.

十二奴局 // Twelve Nujus

买牛的银子要石头一样多。	With money as plentiful as stones.

身背晌午饭，　　　　　　With lunch on their backs,
各去一条路，　　　　　　People started off,
买牛来到松格地方。　　　To buy oxen in Songge.

问水牛价钱值多少。　　　They first asked about the price of an ox,
看水牛两角开不开①。　　Checked if the two horns were widely gapped,①
瞧水牛尾巴花不花②。　　And if the tail was mixed in color.②

两只牛角如竹笋，　　　　The two horns looked like bamboo shoots,
大弓一样朝里弯，　　　　Both bending inward like bows;
牛尾上下没有花，　　　　The whole tail was of pure color;
犁田力气大，　　　　　　The ox appeared strong enough,
一根索子拉着就会耙。　　Ready to plow when yoked with a rope,
威咀看着会顺眼，　　　　Weizui would be glad to see it,
实车③望见会喜欢。　　　And Shiche③ was sure to like it.
牛价不高把牛买，　　　　Bought at a low price,
高高兴兴赶回家。　　　　The ox was then led home in excitement.
拉着牛回家的是哪个？　　Who's the one leading it home?

---

① 哈尼族相牛的经验，两只牛角间距离开，认为牛力气小。
② 哈尼族认为牛尾有花则不吉利。
③ 哈尼族传说中管庄稼的神。

① The Hani believe that the closer the gap between the horns, the stronger the ox.
② The Hani believe that it is not auspicious for an ox to have a mix-colored tail.
③ The Hani god in charge of crops.

伙及拉及
Huojilaji

拉着牛回家的是跛脚里德。	Lide the Lame led it home.

松格梁子的牛在不惯高山，   But the hills disagreed with the ox from Songge,
买来几天就死了；   Which died a few days later;
犁田耙田的尖角牛死了，   Now the plowing ox was dead,
男人老实着急，   The men became really anxious.
二天敬献威咀的饭，   They made offerings to Weizui two straight days,
没有牛来犁田怎样栽？   There can be no planting without the ox plowing;
二天敬献实车的饭，   They made offerings to Shiche two straight days,
没有牛来耙田怎样种？   There can be no farming without the ox raking.

请问寨中的长老，   The respected elders in the village were consulted:
松格买来的牛死了，   Now the ox from Songge is dead,
犁田耙田的牛哪里去找？   Where can a new one be found?
白宏[①]埕玛[②]有牛卖，   In Diema[①] where the Baihong[②] live,
一头牛要两头牛的价钱，   Oxen were for sale at a doubled price,
买牛的银子要石头一样多。   Which cost money as plentiful as stones.

请问白宏埕玛的牛主人，   They asked the ox owner in Diema:
牛的价钱要多少？   How much is your ox?
牛身子多大，   Though it's a heavy ox,
不能要牛身子重的钱；   It's unfair to charge money of equal weight;

---

① 白宏：哈尼族的一个支系。   ① A place in Honghe County.
② 埕玛：地名，在红河县境内。   ② A branch of the Hani people.

十二奴局 // Twelve Nujus

牛毛有多少根，	Though it had countless hairs,
不能要牛毛一样多的钱。	It's unfair to charge money of equal amount.
买卖双方不吃亏，	Let's make a fair deal,
牛价给你银子四五钱。	At the price of five silver coins.

兑了银子买成牛，　　　　The deal was completed,
拉着耕牛转回家，　　　　And they led the ox home.
吆喝耕牛快快走，　　　　They hastened the ox loudly,
早早回家犁田耙田。　　　In order to start plowing and raking quickly.

挖田的人，　　　　　　　Farming people,
四个眼的犁快安好，　　　Get the four-shifted plow ready,
九个齿的木耙快修理。　　And the nine-toothed rake fixed.
犁田要犁三回，　　　　　Three times you shall plow the field.
耙田要耙三道，　　　　　Three times you shall rake the field.
威咀吃的谷米要栽出来，　In this way the corn to be offered
实车吃的谷米要栽出来。　To Weizui and Shiche are produced.

布谷叫了，　　　　　　　Cuckoos chirping,
春耕时节来到；　　　　　It's time for spring plowing;
燕子叫了，　　　　　　　Swallows singing,
安排农活的时节来到。　　It's time for farm work.
田里的水一天比一天变热了，As the paddy water gets hotter and hotter,
男人女人赶快去下田。　　Men and women go farming now!

伙及拉及
Huojilaji

众：萨—萨！　　　　　　　Chorus: Sah-Sah!

二　月

The Second Month

萨啦阿依——　　　　　　　Sala Ayi–
旧的一月过去，　　　　　　The old month has gone by,
新的一月来到。　　　　　　And the new one comes.
山上的桃花开了，　　　　　The peach blossoms in the mountains,
寨边的染饭花香了。　　　　And the air is scented with the maxim flower.
女人织布忙，　　　　　　　Women are busy weaving,
家家织机"滴答"响；　　　 With looms ticking in every household;
男人犁田不知太阳落山，　　Men kept plowing despite the sunset,
烧起篝火歇田房①。　　　　 And lit bonfires to spend the night in the field.
不是过年的时候，　　　　　It is not the time of the New Year,
要染黄糯米过一回节。　　　But the glutinous rice is to be dyed yellow like during festivals.

高山上撒荞子的时节到了，　It's time for buckwheat seeding on the hill;
河坝里栽棉花的时节到了，　It's time for cotton planting down by the dam.
背肥的女人不歇脚，　　　　Women spare no effort carrying manure,
像采花的蜜蜂出出进进。　　Like honeybees busy picking flowers;
砍地的男人，　　　　　　　Men go to open up the land,

---

① 歇田房：即吃住在田房的意思。

十二奴局 // Twelve Nujus

左手拿钩把①，	With bamboo hooks in their left hands,
右手把弯刀握得紧紧，	And machetes firm in their right hands,
砍倒刺丛杂草。	Clearing all the barbed weeds.
挖田的男人，	Farming men,
忙得淌汗的时节来到了，	It is now the time of sweating:
一天干十天吃的日子，	One day's labor will ensure ten days' food.
挥动亮闪闪的大锄头，	With bright hoes shining in their hands,
泥水沾脸不怕，	Faces muddied;
挖断土狗、蚯蚓的头不怕，	Despite the earthworms dug up
挖断泥鳅、黄鳝的腰不怕，	Or the loaches and eels stirred,
你挖我不停，	You just compete with each other
我挖你不闲。	Digging and farming.

布谷鸟叫了，	Cuckoos cooing,
春耕的时间来到；	It's now time for spring plowing;
燕子叫了，	Swallows chirping,
催生产的日子来到。	It's time for farming.
汉人下种的季节到了，	When the Han do the sowing,
哈尼栽秧的季节快来了。	And the Hani spread the seeds.
寨边的小秧盖满秧田水，	The fields are now covered with seedlings,
嫩汪汪像床缘行毯；	Tender and soft like blankets on the beds.
秧苗望着山下了，	They see their future down the hill,

---

① 砍草用的竹木工具。

伙及拉及
Huojilaji

等着要嫁大田①了。
弟兄不分家会在一处，
谷秧不分家不会在一处。
众：萨—萨！

Where the large fields are waiting for their arrival.
Brothers stay with each other unless divided,
While seedlings grow together only after separation.
Chorus: Sah-Sah!

三　月

The Third Month

萨啦阿依——
旧的一月过去了，
新的一月来到。
勤劳的伙子，
挖田地的男人，
快上山砍锥栗木，
修理九齿木耙；
快下箐扯老藤子，
扭成牢牢的耙索；
架起弯角的牨子牛，
耙田要耙三回。
一天干十天吃的日子，
吃奶的小牛叫娘不要心疼，
三岁的小牛上耙不要手软，
九岁的老牛上耙不要心软。
满月的小娃，

Sala Ayi–
The old month has gone by,
And the new one comes.
Industrious young men,
Who earn a living by farm work,
Go cut chestnut wood up on the hills,
And fix your nine-toothed rakes;
Pull down the rattans down in the valley,
And twist them into firm ropes,
With which the oxen with bending horns are yoked,
To rake the fields three times.
One day's labor will ensure ten days' food,
So no hard feelings when the calves are mooing for their moms;
No hard feelings when three-year-old calves are hitched;

---

① 嫁大田：即栽秧。

十二奴局 // Twelve Nujus

一天变一个样；	No hard feelings when nine-year-old oxen are yoked.
弟兄不分家会在一处，	A baby one month old
秧田不分家不会在一处，	Will grow and change constantly;
秧苗姑娘长大，	Brothers stay with each other unless divided,
要嫁婆家了。	While seedlings grow together only after separation.
耙田过后三天，	As the girls of the seedlings grow up,
欢欢喜喜开秧门。	It's time for them to get married.
勤劳的女人，	Three days after the fields are raked,
半夜起来烧火煮饭，	The covered seedlings are to be revealed.
床上娃娃蹬开被窝忙不得看，	Hardworking women
腰带散落地上顾不得管，	Get up to cook in the middle of the night,
栽秧吃的饭菜煮好了，	Despite the blankets kicked off by the kids,
公鸡还未跳出窝。	Or the belts scattered on the ground.
	When the food for the day is ready,
	The roosters are yet to jump out of their nests.
栽秧要先栽三耙，	Of the first three rakes of seedlings,
不是我家先栽秧①，	We are neither the first[①],
不是我家后栽秧②。	Nor the last to plant[②].
先栽的头把秧，	The first rake of the seedlings
是人的面份；	Is for people;

---

① 哈尼族旧有最先栽秧不吉利的说法。
② 哈尼族认为后栽秧是对神的不恭。

① The Hani believe that it is not auspicious to be the first one to plant.
② The Hani believe that it is disrespectful to the gods if they are the last one to plant.

伙及拉及
Huojilaji

中间栽的第二把秧，	The second rake
是庄稼的面份，	For the crops;
后栽的第三把秧，	The last rake
是牛马牲畜的面份。	For cattle and horses.
栽秧要用什么献？	What is to be offered to the gods before the planting?
要染黄糯米饭敬献，	Glutinous rice dyed yellow,
要染红鸡蛋来敬献。	And eggs dyed red.
栽秧的日子，	On the day of planting,
田坝像赶街子一样热闹：	The fields are crowded like a fair:
阿爸阿妈来栽秧，	With dads and moms planting,
兄弟姐妹来栽秧，	Brothers and sisters planting,
亲戚朋友来栽秧。	Relatives and friends planting.
彝家栽秧的日子，	It's the planting day for the Yi people;
傣家栽秧的日子，	It's the planting day for the Dai people;
哈尼栽秧的日子。	It's the planting day for the Hani people.
阿爸阿妈不要害羞，	Be proud of yourselves my mom and dad;
哥哥姐姐不要害羞。	Be proud of yourselves my dear siblings.
你栽秧我不歇手，	I will not stop when you plant,
我栽秧你不闲着。	And you don't slack off when I sow.
威咀吃的栽下了，	Offerings for Weizui are now planted;
实车吃的栽下了，	Offerings for Shiche are now sown.
一季栽秧一年粮。	One season's labor will yield a year's food.
众：萨—萨！	Chorus: Sah-Sah!

十二奴局 // Twelve Nujus

四 月

The Fourth Month

萨啦阿依——
旧的一月过去了，
新的一月来到。
梨树结出嫩嫩的绿果，
仰阿娜①的日子来到了。

低洼的地方有千百处，
最低的是河水淌的地方；
高高的山峰有千座万座，
最高的是孟资山②。
地上大大小小动物出来游，
天上星星斗斗出来游；
山头的妥底玛依开放，
山沟的索都扎依③开放。
女人的包头角，
像老鹰翅膀扇动，
姑娘身上的腰带亮闪闪，

---

① 仰阿娜：哈尼族叶车人的一个传统活动，在每年农历四月水田栽插禾苗后举行。"仰阿娜"即休息之意。
② 在红河县境内。
③ 一种山杜鹃花。

Sala Ayi–
The old month has gone by,
And the new one comes.
Pear trees bear tender green fruit,
Now it's time for the Yang'ana① Festival.

Among thousands of low-lying places,
The lowest is the place where the river flows;
Among thousands of high mountains,
The highest is Mount Mengzi②.
Animals large and small, roam on the ground,
While stars in all sizes wander in the sky.
The azaleas are in full bloom uphill,
And rhododendrons are in flower down in the ravine.
Women's headscarves
Sway like eagle wings;
Girls' belts are dazzling,

---

① A Hani festival in the fourth month, meaning "taking a rest".
② In Honghe County.

伙及拉及
Huojilaji

比妥底玛依还漂亮。	Even more attractive than azaleas.
姑娘小伙仰阿娜,	Girls and boys are celebrating Yang'ana;
老人小娃仰阿娜,	Elders and youngsters are celebrating Yang'ana;
村村寨寨仰阿娜,	All villages are celebrating Yang'ana.
敲起牛皮鼓仰阿娜,	Leather drums are beaten,
敲起铓锣仰阿娜,	And gongs struck.
不上山欢乐的人没有了,	All go up the mountain happily,
脸上不见笑的人没有了。	With smiles on their faces.
古时候阿皮拾德棕莫①,	Api Shidezongmo①, our ancestor
站在孟资山上,	Stood on Mount Mengzi,
一眼一眼望下去,	And kept looking down:
傣家地方让它谷子好,	May the crops grow well in the Dai place;
汉人地方让它谷子好;	May the crops grow well in the Han place.
一眼一眼朝上看去,	She then kept looking up:
高山的荞子让它饱满,	May the buckwheat grow full;
五谷是人不死的药。	May the grain feed all the people.
四月到了,	Here comes the fourth month,
田地等着要梳头了,	And the fields are waiting to have their hair combed;

---

① 阿皮,对老年妇女的尊称;拾德棕莫,哈尼族传说中最先仰阿娜的女祖先。

① Api, an honorific for elderly women. Shidezongmo, the female ancestor of the Hani who started the Yang'ana festival.

- 203 -

十二奴局 // Twelve Nujus

比哭阿妈①飞出来了，
安排女人来薅头道秧。
比哭阿妈住在哪里？
住在墨索②地方。
它从远远的地方叫着来，
催促人们快薅秧。
家里的女人，
丢开吃奶的娃娃，
像鸭子一样钻进田里，
黑草要拔干净，
黄草要拔干净，
你薅秧我不歇手，
我薅秧你不闲着。
众：萨—萨！

The biku'ama bird flies in the sky,
Calling for women to pull weeds.
Where does the bird live?
It lives in the place of Mosuo①.
It calls all the way from the distance,
Urging people to pull weeds.
Women of every household,
Leaving babies they are nursing,
Head into the fields like ducks.
Black weeds are to be pulled out clean;
Yellow weeds are to be pulled out clean.
I won't stop when you are working,
And you don't idle away while I'm laboring.
Chorus: Sah-Sah!

五 月

The Fifth Month

萨啦阿依——
旧的一月过去了，
新的一月来到。
雨水下地了，
竹笋节节冒土了。

Sala Ayi–
The old month has gone by,
And the new one comes.
During the rainy season,
Bamboo shoots are sprouting.

---

① 比哭阿妈：一种小鸟。
② 古地名。

① An ancient place.

伙及拉及
Huojilaji

一年不满过第三次年的日子来了，	It's the third time to celebrate the New Year.
"矻扎"的时节来了。	Here comes the Kezha Festival.
威咀不请自己来，	When Weizui arrives uninvited,
实车不请自己来，	And Shiche descends unasked.
威咀要来看山寨，	Weizui means to watch out for the villages,
实车要来保庄稼。	And Shiche to look after the crops.
砍棵直直的松树安磨秋，	Cut down a straight pine tree as the Moqiu Pole,
背来绿绿的松枝撒马路①。	And pave green pine needles on the road①.
好马忘不了走过的路，	A good horse will never forget the road it has been through,
哈尼人忘不了磨秋场。	And the Hani cannot live without the Moqiu Square.
七十岁的老人来了，	Seventy-year-olds come;
三岁的小娃来了，	Three-year-olds come;
小伙子一对对骑磨秋，	Young men ride the Moqiu in pairs,
小姑娘一个一个打秋千。	While girls play on the swings one by one.
秋千高高地飞，	The high flying swing
把病害甩开；	Gets rid of all diseases;
磨秋团团地转，	Spinning Moqiu
把魔鬼撵走。	Expels the devil.
男人女人平平安安，	Men and women get peace,
大寨小寨热热闹闹。	And all the villages are full of life.

---

① 松枝撒马路：表示迎接威咀神的意思。　① Pine needles spread on the road means a grand ceremony in reception of the god.

放倒磨秋吹热风，
水田要薅第二道草。
薅红草不留根，
薅黑草不留根，
看去秧苗绿油油，
家家户户心喜欢。
众：萨—萨！

Put down the Moqiu Pole in the hot breeze,
Now it's time to pull the weeds again.
Red weeds are to be uprooted;
Black weeds are to be uprooted.
Now the fields are lush green,
And all the people are contented.
Chorus: Sah-Sah!

六 月

The Sixth Month

萨啦阿依——
旧的一月过去了，
新的一月来到。
树林里达优①鸣叫了，
秧棵的肚子圆圆打苞了。
雷，你不要打，
雨，你不要下，
风，你不要刮，
让秧棵平安生长。

家里的男人，
不要四处窜玩，

Sala Ayi–
The old month has gone by,
And the new one comes.
Cicadas in the woods are chirping,
And the grain is now forming ears.
Thunder, please refrain from striking;
Rain, please refrain from falling;
Wind, please refrain from blowing,
So that the grain can grow safely.

Men from every household,
Stop fooling around.

---

① 哈尼语，即蝉子。

伙及拉及
Huojilaji

快磨亮甩草刀，	Grind your knives,
去砍净田边的杂草；	And cut clean the weeds by the fields;
快扛起锄头，	Pick up your hoes,
去把田埂铲光滑。	And go level the ridges.
铲下杂草沤肥料，	As the weeds are shoveled and turned into manure,
老鼠不敢来做窝，	Mice are kept from nesting,
害虫不敢来吃秧。	And pests from eating.
杀只小鸡祭谷神，	Chickens killed are offered to the god of grain,
谷神长在秧苗旺。	Who will bless us with a bumper harvest.
众：萨—萨！	Chorus: Sah-Sah!

七 月　　The Seventh Month

萨啦阿依——	Sala Ayi–
旧的一月过去了，	The old month has gone by,
新的一月来到。	And the new one comes.
七月吹热风，	In the hot breeze of the seventh month,
谷子抽穗谷花香。	Millet is in ears fragrant;
达优处处叫了，	Cicadas are singing here and there,
一年的粮挂到嘴边了；	And a year's food is now within reach.
勤劳的男人，	Industrious men,
快拿起七尺长的竹刀，	Pick up your bamboo knives seven feet long,
砍倒田埂上的茅草；	And cut down the grass on the ridges;
快去砍来木条子，	Go to cut wood strips,

修理漏雨的田房。	And repair the leaking cottage in the fields.
七月吃新谷①的节气来到了，	July sees the New Grain Festival①,
挖来甜甜的竹笋，	When sweet bamboo shoots are dug out,
摘来嫩嫩的豆荚，	Fresh pods collected,
炸出白生生的米花，	White rice fried,
再祭一次谷神。	And the god of grain honored.
雷，不要惊跑谷魂，	Thunder, please do not scare away the grain soul;
雨，不要冲走谷魂，	Rain, please do not wash away the grain soul;
风，不要吹散谷魂，	Wind, please do not blow away the grain soul.
愿谷子的脸转向寨子，	May the grain all face the village,
望着哈尼的大门。	Gazing at the gate of the Hani.
众：萨—萨！	Chorus: Sah-Sah!

八 月

The Eighth Month

萨啦阿依——
旧的一月过去了，
新的一月来到。
达优不停地叫，
达优催秋收的时节到了。

Sala Ayi–
The old month has gone by,
And the new one comes.
Cicadas kept creaking,
Suggesting the time of autumn harvest.

谷穗弯腰了，
谷子要回家了。

Ears of corn stoop down,
And the grain is ready to go home.

---

① 哈尼族的一个传统节日。

① A traditional festival of the Hani people.

伙及拉及
Huojilaji

勤劳的男人，	Industrious men,
快把打谷船①收好，	Get your boat-shaped threshers ready,
沟上的木桥要加固，	The wooden bridge over the gully reinforced,
进村的大路要修宽；	And the road to the village widened;
勤劳的女人，	Hardworking women,
快缝补装粮的麻袋，	Get the grain sacks mended,
快准备割谷的锯镰。	And the harvesting scythes ready.

栽在河坝的棉花开了，　　　As the cotton plants along the dam bloom,
快背上布包拾棉花；　　　　Go pick them with your bags;
种在山梁上的高粱红了，　　As the sorghum on the ridges turns red,
快背着背篓去采；　　　　　Go collect them with baskets on your back;
梯田里的谷子黄了，　　　　As the corn in the terraces grows yellow,
汗水淌出来的粮食到口了，　Food from hard labor is now within reach,
哈尼像蜜蜂忙的日子来到了！And here come the days when the Hani are busy like bees!

锯镰快快地割，　　　Cut fast with scythes,
谷船重重地打，　　　And spare no efforts threshing,
你割谷我不歇手，　　I will not stop when you are cutting,
我打谷你不松闲，　　And you don't slack off when I'm threshing.
庄稼收到家，　　　　When the crops are harvested,
杀一只母鸡，　　　　A hen will be killed,

---

① 打谷子的用具，形如船状。

十二奴局 // Twelve Nujus

杀一只公鸡，	Together with a rooster;
蒸一甑糯米饭，	A pot of glutinous rice will be steamed,
祭献守仓的谷神。	And offered to the god of grain.
众：萨—萨！	Chorus: Sah-Sah!

九 月 / The Ninth Month

萨啦阿依——
旧的一月过去了，
新的一月来到。
样样庄稼收回来了，
家里粮仓满满的了。

Sala Ayi–
The old month has gone by,
And the new one comes.
All the crops are now harvested;
The granaries are now full.

勤劳的人，
吃着新米要想着明年。
锄头要加钢，
趁天热好挖田；
你挖我不歇手，
我挖你不松闲。
搭好骡子背一样的埂子，
挖过头道田，
哈尼要过十月年①。

Industrious men
Think of next year when enjoying the fresh rice.
Hoes are to be sharpened,
And put to farm work during the warm days.
I won't rest when you are laboring,
And you don't slack off when I'm working.
As the ridges are consolidated like mule backs,
And soil dug up for the first time,
The Hani are ready to celebrate the New Year①.

---

① 哈尼族历法将十月定为岁首。十月年是哈尼族最盛大的节日。

① The Hani people take the tenth month as the end of a year, so Festival of the Tenth Month is the grandest festival.

伙及拉及
Huojilaji

众：萨—萨！　　　　　　Chorus: Sah-Sah!

十　月　　　　　　　　The Tenth Month

萨啦阿依——　　　　　　Sala Ayi–
旧的一年过去，　　　　　The old year has gone by,
新的一年来到。　　　　　And the new one comes.
最后的一日翻过来了，　　Now the last day has passed;
最后的一月翻过来了。　　The last month has gone.
住河坝的傣家，　　　　　The Dai living along the river dam
有自己过年的日子，　　　Have their own New Year's Day.
住大寨子的汉人，　　　　The Han living in large villages
有自己过年的日子；　　　Have their own New Year's Day,
不是山上的树没有脚，　　Unlike the footless trees in the hills,
哈尼也有过年的时候。　　The Hani also have their own New Year's Day.
哈尼的年哪时过？　　　　When do the Hani celebrate their New Year?
年头年尾怎样分？　　　　When do they end a year and start a new one?
哈尼过年在十月间，　　　The Hani celebrate their New Year in the tenth month,
吃新谷饭的那天算一年。　On the day when they eat the newly harvested rice.
最先吃年饭的是哪个？　　Who was the first to host New Year's dinner parties?
最先吃年饭的是腊咪阿母①。Lami'amu① was the first to host those parties.
最先踩粑粑的是哪个？　　Who was the first to make rice cakes?

---

① 腊咪阿母：哈尼族传说中的一　① A female ancestor of the Hani.
　个女祖先。

十二奴局 // Twelve Nujus

最先踩粑粑的是欧红然依①。	Ouhongranyi① was the first to make rice cakes.
叶车最先煮年饭的是哪个？	Who was the first Yeche to cook the New Year dinner?
是阿皮火白火谷② 阿妈。	Api Huobaihuogu② was the first to cook it.
花开有最好的一朵，	Of the blooming flowers there is one prettiest,
一日有最好的时辰，	Of the hours of a day there is one best.
哈尼过年哪天日子好？	Which is the best day for the Hani New Year?
属兔的日子最好；	The Day of the Rabbit is the best.
天神保平安，	With blessings from
地神保平安，	Heavenly and earthly gods,
寨神保平安，	As well as village gods,
寨寨热热闹闹，	Every village is full of life;
家家喜喜欢欢。	Every household is happy.
众：萨—萨！	Chorus: Sah-Sah!

---

① 欧红然依：哈尼族传说中的一个女祖先。
② 火白火谷：哈尼族传说中的一个女祖先。

① A female ancestor of the Hani.
② A female ancestor of the Hani.

About the Translator

Wang Lei is currently a lecturer in the School of Foreign Languages and Literature at Yunnan Normal University. She's been teaching English and doing research in translation and writing for over 15 years. Her recent publications include one book: *Teaching College English Writing in the Technology Environment*, and two journal articles: "Applied Terminology from the Cognitive Perspective" and "Memory Resources Management in Interpretation".